FAIR FLOWER OF NORTHUMBERLAND

Amanda believes that Justin is cold-bloodedly planning to marry her step-sister for her money. She allows him only one good quality: he is clever, especially at putting her in the wrong. When she is forced to revise her opinion, she admits that she judged too hastily — but the last thing she expected was to find herself fathoms deep in love with the object of her distrust . . .

Books by Harriet Smith
in the Linford Romance Library:

AUSTRALIAN NURSE

HARRIET SMITH

$\blacklozenge$

FAIR FLOWER OF NORTHUMBERLAND

Complete and Unabridged

LINFORD
Leicester

First published in Great Britain in 1975 by
Robert Hale Limited
London

First Linford Edition
published 2014
by arrangement with
Robert Hale Limited
London

A catalogue record for this book is available
from the British Library.

ISBN 978–1–4448–1938–0

Published by
F. A. Thorpe (Publishing)
Anstey, Leicestershire

Set by Words & Graphics Ltd.
Anstey, Leicestershire
Printed and bound in Great Britain by
T. J. International Ltd., Padstow, Cornwall

This book is printed on acid-free paper

1

Greystones Cottage fitted its name, and the Northumbrian hills amongst which it was set. It was smallish, plain, and built of solid grey stone. To Amanda, it looked homelike and welcoming, at the end of a long, hot journey. She was a trifle less certain of her welcome indoors. As she shut the front door, and dumped her case down, her step-mother appeared in the kitchen doorway. 'Amanda! We weren't expecting you until next week!'

'I just suddenly made up my mind to come today.'

'Well, you might have rung up. You know how far we are from shops.'

'I'm not fussy. I'll eat cheese and biscuits, if we're short,' returned Amanda blithely. 'I told you, I decided at the last moment. The country's nicer than the town, in this weather.'

'How on earth did you get here, with

1

your luggage? One of us would have met you.'

'I meant to leave my case with Mrs Barlowe, and walk. As it happened, I didn't have to. Randall Warren came past the bus-stop, just after I'd got off, and offered me a lift.'

'Randall Warren,' repeated Mrs Carr slowly. 'I didn't think you knew any of the Warrens.'

'I don't. I know Randall by sight, and apparently he knows who I am. Why did no one tell me that Vanessa was engaged to his brother?'

'Because she wanted to tell you herself, of course. She wouldn't tell anyone, except the Warrens and ourselves, until you came home. It's a pity Randall got in first.'

Amanda refrained from saying that it was news of Vanessa's engagement which had brought her home in such a hurry, news heard from someone who belonged to neither family. She was fond of her step-mother. They got on excellently most of the time, and

Amanda never resented the fact that Mrs Carr's own daughter came first with her. After all, her father loved his own daughter best. None the less, it was that daughter, Vanessa, who was the one real bone of contention between Amanda and her step-mother. 'Where is Vanessa?' she asked.

'Out somewhere with Justin. She won't be back for two or three hours. Your father's in the garden.'

'I want a wash first, then I'll go out to him.'

Half an hour later, feeling considerably cleaner and cooler, Amanda sat at her window, overlooking the back garden. It was a large garden, and somewhat untidy, as the Carrs were spasmodic gardeners, rather than real enthusiasts. Lifting her eyes beyond the garden walls, she looked with delight at the high, lonely Northumberland fells. She was an almost aggressively north-country girl. It was only a year since they had come to this cottage, after years of living in a midland town, but already it seemed more fully home to her than any other house she could remember.

She ran downstairs. Her step-mother called from the kitchen that she was just taking tea into the garden, so would Amanda carry some of it. Together, they went down to the little stone summer-house at the bottom of the garden. Mr Carr pushed his books and papers aside, and gave his daughter a welcome whose warmth left nothing to be desired.

'Of course it's nice to have you home a few days early,' said Mrs Carr, pouring out tea. 'Vanessa will be delighted, but she *will* be disappointed that Randall's told you about her engagement, when she was keeping it for a surprise. How did you like him?'

'Randall? I'm not sure. He's friendly enough, and very good-looking.'

'So is Justin, though they're not at all alike. You've never seen him?' Amanda shook her head. 'No, he's only been here since his father was ill, in the spring. We all like him, and of course the Warrens are one of the oldest families in Northumberland.'

The smug satisfaction of this remark pricked Amanda into saying: 'I hope that isn't why Vanessa accepted him.'

'Don't be silly, of course it isn't. But most people would think it an added attraction.'

'I wouldn't. We all go back to the cave-men, so how can any one family be older than others?' said Amanda, combatively.

Her father laughed, but her step-mother gave her an annoyed look. 'I hope you're not going to be prejudiced against Justin just because he *is* a Warren. If so, Vanessa will be upset. She's very much in love.'

If Amanda was only fond of her step-mother, she really loved her step-sister. Both only children, she and Vanessa had been delighted to adopt each other as sisters, and had always been the best of friends. Vanessa was as good-humoured as she was pretty, but a little too pliant and suggestible, very easily influenced by more determined characters. Too often, she was pulled in one direction by her mother, and then in the opposite one by Amanda, so that it was difficult to be sure which was the real Vanessa. Amanda believed that Mrs Carr had a bad influence on Vanessa. Mrs Carr allowed that Amanda was cleverer than her own daughter, but sometimes had an unfortunate influence over her. So today, as often before, there was a faint light of battle in their eyes, when they spoke of Vanessa.

When Mrs Carr wheeled the tea-trolley back to the house, Amanda did not offer to help with the washing-up. It seemed far too good an opportunity for a private gossip with her father. She sat on the summer-house step, the family cat on one side, Vanessa's black poodle on the other, rather absently answering her father's questions about her doings. After a while he stopped, looked at her lively, expressive face, and said: 'You're very put out about Vanessa's engagement, aren't you? Why, when you don't even know Justin?'

'I can't understand Vanessa's keeping me so much in the dark about it. That's not like her. She's never even mentioned Justin's name. How long has she known him?'

'Since he came up here, two or three months ago. She's been friendly with the other two, Randall and Caroline, since she met them at a party, last winter. They asked her to a party at Danesford, afterwards.'

'I've never been invited to a Danesford party.'

'Anyone would think you were jealous, if they didn't know you,' commented Mr Carr, amused.

'*Real* friends don't treat us differently, just because Vanessa has money, and I haven't. The Warrens may be one of the oldest families in the county, but I've heard they're on the rocks, financially.'

'In difficulties, perhaps. But they own a lot of land, and land has increased in value.'

'And it would be a pity to sell valuable land, which may become more valuable. Much wiser to marry for money.'

'I rather like Justin,' remarked Mr Carr, mildly. 'He's not exactly easy to know, but I like him. He's intelligent, and very knowledgeable about local history.'

'Oh!' said Amanda, very expressively. Her father had been retired rather early, when his company had been taken over by a larger one. Having a reasonable pension, he had decided not to try for another job, but to return to his native county, and occupy his leisure by writing a history of Northumberland. Amanda doubted if it would ever be published, but the reading, writing and exploring kept him very happily occupied. Anyone who had an interest in the subject, or pretended an interest, had a flying start with him. She got up. 'Mother says Vanessa won't be back until later, so I think I'll take Blackie for a walk.'

Chance brought her home at exactly the right moment. A car had just drawn up at the gate. Two people got out, one of them Vanessa. It wasn't until she had almost reached them that Vanessa turned, and saw Amanda. Astonishment, pleasure, and then a little doubt crossed her face in rapid succession. 'Amanda! When did you get back? Why didn't you let anyone know you were coming today?'

'I only decided late last night.'

Amanda glanced from Vanessa to her companion. Vanessa hastily introduced them: 'You've not met Justin Warren, Amanda.' She gave him a warning glance as she spoke.

Amanda easily interpreted this as an order not to mention their engagement. She gave Justin a cool, firm hand, and a long, cool look. 'Your brother gave me a lift, and told me that you were engaged to Vanessa.'

This brought an exclamation of vexation from Vanessa. Justin took Amanda's hand, and gave her an equally cool, and measuring glance, seeing a slim girl of medium height, bright hazel eyes under chestnut hair, an irregular but attractive face, and a sprinkling of freckles over her short, charming nose.

Amanda's critical eyes took in a tall, spare young man, good-looking in a restrained fashion, with dark grey eyes under well-marked brows. He wasn't in the least like his brother, she decided. Randall was lively and boyish, while Justin had an impassive, and rather severe expression. A small smile touched his lips briefly, and then vanished. 'I've heard a lot about you from Vanessa,' he told her. 'I expect we'll be seeing a good deal of each other.'

'Probably. I'll be here until the end of September.'

'Well, I expect you and Vanessa will have plenty to talk about, so I won't stay. Perhaps Vanessa will bring you to Danesford to meet the rest of us, some time soon.'

Justin turned away, and the girls went

indoors together. 'Come up to my room,' said Vanessa. 'Did you have to be so cool to Justin?' she complained, as she shut the door.

'I didn't mean to be, but we are total strangers,' said Amanda reasonably. 'You might give me time to get to know him, and to recover from the surprise of your engagement.'

'I intended to tell you the minute you came home. I couldn't have known you'd hear it from Randall first. Surely you understand?'

'Yes, of course.'

'Then why do you keep on sounding so annoyed?' demanded Vanessa in exasperated tones.

Without answering, Amanda sat down on the end of the bed. There was a question in her eyes, and a slight wariness in Vanessa's. There was six months between them in age. Vanessa was just turned twenty, Amanda a little short of it. They had lived as sisters for the last ten years, had squabbled, argued and had crazes together; experimented, and made asses of themselves. The bond between them was so strong that they rarely remembered that there was no blood tie, but it showed in their lack of any physical resemblance. Vanessa was the prettier of the two, a small, neatly made girl, with very blue eyes, black hair and a pale skin. Amanda was a little taller, and her charm lay, not in the regularity of her features, but in the sparkle and animation of her hazel eyes, a mouth that was full and generous and inclined to laughter, and an impulsive grace of movement.

'If I am annoyed,' she said slowly, 'you should know why. You've never even mentioned Justin's name to me. And not so long ago you were fathoms deep in love with Richard Bolton.'

Quick colour ran up Vanessa's cheeks. 'That's more than a year ago,' she exclaimed vehemently. 'People change. You should know that. You've been in and out of love with at least half a dozen people in the last few years.'

'Not more than four,' Amanda corrected her. 'And I was only half-way in love, and then realized I didn't really want to go the whole way. It didn't seem like that with you and Richard.'

'He means nothing to me now, absolutely nothing. Nor I to him.'

'I see. So that's why you told his sister about your engagement, before telling me?'

Vanessa put her hand to her mouth, in an unconsciously caught out gesture. She stared at Amanda, then exclaimed: 'So that's why you came home so suddenly! You knew before you met Randall.' Amanda nodded, and Vanessa hurried on: 'I wanted to tell you all about it when you came home, and I told the Warrens that no one outside the family must be told, until you got back. Only I just happened to be writing to Anne, and it never occurred to me that you might meet her.' This explanation sounded a bit lame, even to Vanessa. She hastily changed the subject. 'Do you like Justin?'

'How can I say, when we only saw each other for a couple of minutes?

Isn't he a bit old for you?'

'He's only twenty-seven,' Vanessa protested.

'Is that all?' Amanda's eyebrows shot up in surprise. 'I thought he was at least thirty. A very middle-aged young man!'

'Honestly, Amanda!' Vanessa turned away with an angry flounce. 'You seem determined to dislike Justin, probably just because he's a Warren of Danesford. You're an inverted snob.'

'That's Mother's phrase, not yours,' retorted Amanda shrewdly. 'I'm not as unreasonable as all that. If Justin was a nobody, I wouldn't be wondering if you were attracted by the idea of becoming Mrs Warren of Danesford. And if the Warrens weren't hard-up, I wouldn't be wondering if he's marrying you for your money.'

'It's not very flattering to suggest that my money's my only recommendation.' Vanessa looked at her face in the mirror, and then smiled. 'Believe me, Amanda, I'm very much in love with Justin. As to Danesford, it's the loveliest place, and I'm sure you'll agree, when you see it. I'd have thought, being so mad about Northumberland, you'd have been thrilled to be connected with a family who've lived here for hundreds of years, and who have links with most of the famous Border families, including the Percys. I think that's something to be proud of.'

'Now, you're just play-acting,' said Amanda.

At this, Vanessa lost her temper completely. 'You're quite insufferable; smug, self-righteous, and bossy,' she flared. 'Well, you can't boss me any longer. As you're determined to be unpleasant, I'm going.'

She slammed the door behind her. Amanda looked after her without offence. They had said worse things to one another in the past, and she knew Vanessa would soon forget her huff. But on other counts, she felt a little uncertain. She had felt sure that Vanessa had been in love with Richard only a year ago, and fairly sure she had not forgotten him. Yet Vanessa had taken the mention of Richard with no more than a certain embarrassment, and then gone up like a rocket at the accusation of play-acting. Perhaps that was because there was more truth in the second accusation.

Vanessa had always wanted to be an actress, with no greater assets than a lovely face and figure, and a very slight talent. If she had possessed sufficient determination, she would probably have become a hard-up, third-rate actress; but Vanessa lacked that sort of driving ambition and determination. Parents and teachers had combined to tell her that she would never be a successful actress, so she had given in, and looked for some duller way to earn a living. Amanda intended to go to a university, so Vanessa decided to go with her. Unfortunately, she was less good at passing exams, so she took a secretarial training instead.

In the ordinary way, Amanda would have gone to their local university, and continued to live at home, but by then her father knew that he would soon become redundant, and had decided to move to Northumberland. So Amanda had chosen to go to Newcastle University, which was near enough for her to go home for week-ends, once the family had moved north.

She knew that Vanessa had hated this separation, feeling that she had been left behind, with no interest except training for a career that was not even second-best, but only third-best. It was about this time that she had become friends with Anne Bolton, and then with her brother Richard. Vanessa had never been short of admirers, but never particularly interested in any of them before. Very soon, Richard had become her closest friend, and constant escort. He was a medical student, two years older than Vanessa, and her mother had looked on their friendship with approval, until the death of Vanessa's uncle, the brother of Mrs Carr's first husband.

He was a widower without children,

living in Australia. Although he had never seen Vanessa, she was his only relative, and years previously he had said that whatever he had when he died would go to Vanessa. No one took this very seriously. He was not even very old. It was a bit of a joke when they were children, and were unable to afford something, to say: 'We'll buy it when Vanessa's uncle leaves her a fortune.' No one could have been more astonished than Vanessa, when her uncle died suddenly, and she found herself heiress to a considerable fortune. And no one could have been less envious than Amanda. Vanessa was generous in her desire to share her good fortune, and they had planned several different ways of enjoying it together, including an exciting holiday abroad.

Somehow, none of these plans had materialized. No one seemed to have got much fun out of the money, thought Amanda. The holiday had been postponed, because of their move to Northumberland. Vanessa had decided not to look for a job that she did not really want. Her capital was in trust until she was twenty-one, or married, but she had more than enough to live on. And her friendship with Richard had come to an abrupt end. What had gone wrong? Amanda wondered. She had always suspected that her step-mother had something to do with it. With all her good qualities, she was a snob, setting a very high value on social prestige, connections, and money, and she had suddenly discovered that Richard's family were nobodys, and that he had a pronounced midland accent.

Had it been only a passing fancy on Vanessa's part, due to loneliness and discontent, which would have come to a natural end, in any case? Had Richard sheered off for fear of being thought a fortune-hunter? Had Vanessa been influenced by her mother into believing that he was no longer good enough for her? Or had Mrs Carr warned him off, in a fashion so hurtful to his pride that

Richard had retired, and never come back? Amanda inclined to this last theory, with no stronger ground than a belief that Vanessa's determined indifference was only skin-deep, that she had been quite badly hurt by Richard's defection. Her letter to Anne Bolton seemed to confirm this; it was so unlike Vanessa to have told a mere friend about her engagement before telling Amanda. She believed that letter had been addressed to Anne, but aimed at Richard, that Vanessa wanted to show him she could do very well without him.

Amanda wished she could be sure that Vanessa had spoken the truth, when she said she was in love with Justin. She sounded as though she meant it, but she possessed enough of the actress to be able to imagine herself into the skin of any part that took her fancy, until she was playing the part almost unconsciously. She might be in love with Justin. Her mother might have persuaded her into believing she loved him. Or she might just be seeing herself in a glamorous new role. Amanda had not taken to Justin at first sight, but if she could be sure that Vanessa really loved him, and that he was not marrying her for gain, she would certainly try to like him. Only it did seem all too *convenient*.

Mrs Warren rang up next day, and asked Vanessa to bring Amanda for tea. An afternoon tea visit did not seem to warrant the amount of fuss Vanessa made about it. 'I've agreed to wear the dress you've chosen,' Amanda said patiently. 'And promised to be on my very best behaviour. Are my manners usually a disgrace?'

'Don't be silly. But you do seem determined to dislike the Warrens. And you're much too fond of saying just what you think.'

Amanda grinned, somewhat ruefully, and made no attempt to deny the charge. Then, seeing Vanessa's worried face, she exclaimed impulsively: 'I promise to do my utmost to like them all, but you can't like people to order. At least, I'll promise to be friendly, whether I like them or not. But I know almost nothing about them, so fill in a few details. Mrs Warren is only Justin's step-mother, isn't she?'

'Yes; his own mother was killed in a car crash, when he was very small. The other two are Mrs Warren's own. Caroline is nineteen, Randall twenty.'

'And what do they do?'

'Randall's just finished at an agricultural college. Caroline doesn't have a job.'

'Just lives to be fashionable and expensive, I suppose?'

There was a touch of sarcasm in Amanda's voice, but Vanessa answered quite mildly: 'I don't have a job either. There aren't very many round here, and her father likes to have her at home. He was very ill in the spring, and is still quite an invalid, so you won't see him today.'

One of the few things Vanessa had done with her money was to buy herself a small car, and in this she drove Amanda to Danesford, a little less than a mile away. Amanda had often passed the gates, but without glimpsing the house, it was so much enclosed by woods. She expected it to be impressive, but was surprised and disarmed to find it quite beautiful. It was long and low, set on a gentle green slope, woods behind, and a shining loop of river at its feet. 'How lovely!' she exclaimed.

Vanessa looked very pleased at this spontaneous tribute. 'It's a Queen Anne house, but built on the site of an earlier one. The Warrens have lived here much longer than that, of course.' There was a glowing satisfaction in her voice, which made Amanda wonder again which she and Justin were most in love with, each other, or each other's possessions.

At that moment, Justin came out to greet them, and Amanda looked at him with wary curiosity. Determined and clever, as well as good-looking, she decided. Those clear, penetrating grey eyes did not go with stupidity, but they were too reserved for her liking. She liked open people, who showed their feelings, and spoke their minds.

Justin took them indoors, and introduced her to Mrs Warren and Caroline. Amanda looked around her with bright-eyed interest. The drawing-room spoke of a luxury and wealth quite new to her, but shyness had been left out of her make-up. Her chief thought was that, if the Warrens were hard-up, this room did not look it, and neither did the two female Warrens. She had not seen Caroline before, and did not take to her. She was a good-looking girl, fair and blue-eyed. She was like Randall in features, but Amanda labelled her a composed, young sophisticate, whereas Randall seemed lively and impulsive, with bold, restless blue eyes, and a mop of wavy, light brown hair tumbling over his forehead. He knew that he was handsome, thought Amanda, and wondered what the two of them thought of Justin's engagement. Did they think he was in love with Vanessa, or doing well for himself, or marrying beneath him?

She glanced at Vanessa, sharing a sofa with Justin. She looked happy and at ease, talking gaily about very little. Justin had almost nothing to say, and Amanda watched him covertly, observing details she had not seen before, a hard, well-knit figure, and a tanned, open-air face, with a firm mouth, a rather hard jaw-line, and a faint scar down one cheek. His expression, and his dark grey eyes were curiously unrevealing, and she remembered her father saying he was not an easy person to know. She was inclined to agree.

The conversation seemed to consist of smooth, trivial courtesies. Amanda was not easily bored, but she was beginning to feel restive, when Justin turned to her, saying: 'I believe you're fond of horses. Would you be interested in seeing ours?'

'I'd love to,' she answered at once. She knew the Warren horses by reputation, but had only seen them in passing, never close to.

Randall accompanied them to the stables. Justin led Amanda round, telling her the names of the horses, and a little about them, and she admired with unfeigned enthusiasm. 'Vanessa's nervous of riding, but says you enjoy it. You're welcome to borrow one of our horses, any time you like,' Justin told her.

It was a generous offer, considering that he did not know how well she could ride, but Amanda was reluctant to accept favours, at least until she knew him better. 'You're very kind,' she answered politely, 'but it's quite a while since I've done any riding, and I doubt if I could manage some of these horses.'

She glanced, as she spoke, at a dark, handsome horse, with a distinctly restive eye. Justin looked slightly amused. 'I certainly wouldn't offer you Sigurd. We've much quieter ones than that.'

'Justin won't allow anyone else to ride that black brute,' chipped in Randall. 'He seems to think no one else could manage him.'

'He doesn't take to strangers. He's been badly handled in the past.'

'I've yet to meet the horse I can't handle,' retorted Randall, combatively.

Justin's mouth tightened. He said nothing, but Amanda felt antagonism quiver in the air between the two brothers. She thought Justin's tone unpleasantly snubbing, but any sympathy she felt for Randall was quenched by the fact that he didn't mind carrying on a family argument in public. She and Vanessa often differed, but not like this, before outsiders. She really had done her best to keep an open mind about the Warrens, but now she was beginning to feel that she could never like any of them.

'Would you like to try one of the quieter horses in the paddock here, tomorrow?' suggested Justin.

'I'll be out all day tomorrow, going to see my grandparents.'

Justin gave her a quick, assessing glance. Amanda's reply had been the simple truth, but she felt that he saw quite clearly the feeling behind it. 'Well, let me know if you change your mind,' he said carelessly, and turned away with Vanessa.

They had said good-bye to the others, before going to the stables, so when they reached Vanessa's car, they only had to say good-bye to Justin and Randall, and drive away. Halfway home, Vanessa stopped, and looked accusingly at Amanda. 'Why did you refuse Justin's offer so brusquely? You know you've often said that you'd love to have a good horse to ride.'

'A horse of my own, but it's quite another thing to borrow someone else's valuable horse. Suppose there was an accident, and the horse was damaged?'

Vanessa sniffed disbelievingly. 'You're a good rider, and know it. The truth is, you don't want to accept a favour from Justin.'

'That was part of it,' Amanda admitted. 'Don't forget Justin's a stranger to me, even though you are engaged to him. Anyone might think twice about accepting an offer of that sort, from someone they don't know.'

'Rubbish! You'd made up your mind to dislike the Warrens, and you showed it,' retorted Vanessa, somewhat unreasonably.

'I tried my best, and I'm sorry if I didn't succeed,' said Amanda, annoyed in her turn. 'I *don't* like the Warrens. I think Mrs Warren and Caroline are patronizing, and Randall shouldn't air family quarrels in public.'

'And Justin?'

'His manners are better than his brother's, but I still don't know him,' answered Amanda, much more carefully. Then with suddenly roused curiosity, she added: 'I thought he had a job somewhere in the south. Is he going to live up here permanently? And where would you be living, when you're married?'

'I don't know, certainly not at Danesford. But it's difficult to get anything settled. Justin did have a job, but he had to come here in the spring, when his father had two bad heart attacks. They were afraid he might not recover. He's much better now, but not well enough to manage the estate. Money worries may have helped to bring on his heart attacks.' So Vanessa did know about the Warrens' money difficulties, thought Amanda. She said nothing and Vanessa went on: 'He's put the management of the estate entirely in Justin's hands, for the time being, but no one knows how long he'll be content with that, so it's very difficult for us to make any plans. Justin decided to resign his job, but says he could probably get a similar one quite easily.'

'What sort of a job?'

'University lecturer, agricultural economics.'

'Oh!' Amanda was a little taken aback, finding it difficult to connect any of the Warrens with such a practical, down-to-earth subject. 'Well, from all I've heard, the estate can do with some agricultural economics. By the way, how did he get that scar on his cheek?'

'I've no idea.' Vanessa sounded surprised. 'I'll ask him, if you're interested.'

'No, no, it was only idle curiosity. But I would have thought — '

Amanda broke off, with a speculative glance at her step-sister. Vanessa coloured hotly, reading the unspoken thought, that any girl really in love would surely have asked that question for herself. She hastily re-started the car, and drove the rest of the way home. 'You can borrow my car, to go to Hesket tomorrow,' she said then.

'That's nice of you. You wouldn't care to come with me? The grand-parents would be delighted to see you.'

'No; I want to take Justin there some day, and introduce him. I'll wait until then.'

The afternoon's visit, though short, had given Amanda plenty to think about. If anything it had increased her doubts about Vanessa's engagement. To begin with, they had been founded only on the obvious fact that marriage to an heiress would be very convenient for Justin Warren, plus a lingering uncertainty about Vanessa's feelings about Richard. But now, she was beginning to dislike Justin, to feel that, whatever Vanessa felt about him, he was not in love with her. His manner was too self-possessed, and much too indifferent. If he really loved Vanessa, he was bound to care something about her sister's opinion. Yet Justin had obviously sensed her own distrust, and equally obviously couldn't care less. Either he was terribly conceited, or quite indifferent to the views of Vanessa's family, and therefore to Vanessa herself.

Was Vanessa in love with him, or merely enjoying one of her glamorous fantasies? Or salving her wounded pride, and paying Richard out for his desertion, by making a grand match? She had not bothered to ask Justin about that scar, though it was something no one could miss, yet nothing to be sensitive about. It rather added to his spare good looks. Surely a girl really in love would want to know everything about the beloved? Amanda certainly would.

2

Amanda set off early next morning, to drive to Hesket Farm, the home of her mother's parents. Mr Deane, an active seventy-six-year-old, had handed the farm over to his son some years earlier, and built a bungalow for himself and his wife, on one corner of the land. Amanda enjoyed her twenty-mile drive over the moors, and received a warm welcome at the end of it. She told them all her news, including Vanessa's engagement. 'Young Warren of Danesford!' exclaimed Mr Deane. 'She's certainly flying high.'

Mrs Carr's satisfaction over her daughter's engagement to a Warren had irritated Amanda, but her grandfather's somewhat similar reaction had no such effect. She knew he had an old-fashioned respect for rank and degree, but only when they included responsibility, as well as privilege; and she had great respect for his judgement. 'Do you know much about the family?' she asked him.

He shook his head. 'Twenty miles is a long way, lass.'

'But you've lived here all your life, and know every farmer in the district. At least, you can tell me one thing, are the Warrens really hard-up?'

'Depends on what you mean by hard-up. They've got a good estate, but it's been bled white for years. If they could sell some of their land, they wouldn't be short of cash; but it's entailed; and I'm told that Justin won't agree to have any of it sold, that he's determined to preserve his inheritance intact. I suppose you're afraid he may be marrying Vanessa for her money. It would certainly come in handy. But Vanessa's a very pretty girl, and money isn't her only attraction.'

'Of course not; but Justin does sound rather a grasping type. Are they good landlords?'

'No.' Mr Deane was very definite on

this point. 'Old Mr Warren, Justin's grandfather, he was well liked. But the present family prefer to spend most of the money on themselves.'

'What do you know about Justin, himself?'

'Nothing, except bits of gossip. He went to school in the south, and hasn't spent very much time at Danesford since he grew up. He's said not to get on with his step-mother and her family. Maybe he doesn't like watching them make the money fly, when he'd rather put it back into the estate.'

'Is Vanessa in love with him?' interjected Mrs Deane.

'She says she is. But I have my doubts.'

'Don't you think she's probably the best judge of that?' Mrs Deane sounded very amused.

'I'm not sure,' answered Amanda thoughtfully. 'I think I know Vanessa better than anyone else, even her mother. She's too easily swept away by anything she thinks romantic and glamorous, and could do with having her feet more firmly on solid ground. She's never known people like the Warrens before, or a house like Danesford. I'm terribly afraid she may be living in a sort of feudal dream, seeing herself married to the handsome young lord of the manor, mistress of a splendid house, and broad acres. There was a boy she seemed to like very much, in Birmingham, before we came here. Something happened to break it up, and now Vanessa swears it was only a passing fancy. But I suspect that Richard still matters a lot to her, and she's using this fairy-tale stuff to try to fill the blank spaces.'

'Isn't it far more likely that she's simply fallen in love with another nice young man?' smiled her grandmother. 'All the Warrens are good-looking, and Vanessa is bound to marry early, with her looks, and no interest in a career. Let them alone, and don't meddle, Amanda.'

Amanda was not convinced that Vanessa did not require to be saved from herself, but she let the subject drop, and enjoyed her day. She had tea at the farmhouse with her uncle's family, and Vanessa's engagement was again discussed with interest, but no one knew much about Justin. 'The young one, Randall, I've seen him ride at Thurston Show,' said one of the boys. 'A dare-devil, if ever there was one, but a fine rider.'

As she was driving home, Amanda noticed a horse and rider on the moor. A moment later, she recognized Randall Warren. Curious about the whole family, she stopped the car, and sat for a while watching him. He was trying to persuade his horse to jump a small stream, and the horse was obviously scared, or reluctant. He would advance almost to the brink, and then come to a dead halt. Each time, with commendable patience, Randall wheeled him round, and tried again. It was a contest of wills, which the man won. The horse finally soared across the water, like a bird, and Amanda involuntarily clapped her hands. Randall turned his head, saw her, and cantered over the rough ground towards her. She got out of the car, and went to meet him. 'I was enjoying the show. You're a grand rider.'

Randall grinned, with a flash of white teeth, and a certain boyish triumph. For the first time, Amanda found herself rather liking him. He slid to the ground, saying: 'I want to ride Thunder at Thurston Show. He's a fine horse, except that he has a thing about crossing water. I'm trying to train him out of it.' Amanda put out a hand to stroke the horse. Randall watched them making friends, a gleam of amusement in his eyes. 'If you're that keen on horses, why did you refuse Justin's offer?'

'Horses can get hurt. I preferred not to risk it, at least until I know him better.'

'Much safer. Justin's altogether too much the economist, and very unforgiving.' Amanda glanced at him sideways, liking him rather less, but sufficiently curious about Justin to want to pick up any scraps of information. She would not question Randall about his brother, but she was quite prepared to listen. But Randall said nothing more on that subject. 'See what you can do with Thunder now,' he suggested. 'He's an easy ride, except for his water phobia. And don't worry, the horses belong to my father, *not* Justin, and Thunder happens to be my own — a birthday present. See if you can get him over that burn.'

Amanda could not resist the challenge. She mounted the horse, and cantered him around the tussocky ground for a while. Then she pulled him up, and took a long look at the burn. 'Are you scared?' grinned Randall.

'Just hoping I don't come off in mid-stream,' she laughed back, and headed the horse for the burn. He took it smoothly, unhesitatingly, like a bird in flight. Amanda drew him to a halt, eyes and cheeks glowing, and Randall applauded generously. She headed the horse back again, and he went flying down the slope, only to slither to such an abrupt halt that she nearly went over his head, into the water. She hauled herself back, thinking that Randall looked rather pleased to see that her initial success had not been repeated. She walked the horse back, and Randall whistled encouragingly to him. Perhaps Thunder realized he would have to cross the burn before he could rejoin his master. He sailed across it, as easily as before, and Amanda slid to the ground. 'He's a beauty, far and away the best horse I've ever ridden.'

'Where did you learn?'

'When I was very small, on my grandfather's farm. He's retired from farming, and my uncle isn't interested in horses, so all I get now is an occasional hired horse.'

'We've other horses as good as Thunder. Why not borrow one, and come for a ride with me? No need to come down to Danesford. I could meet you somewhere up here, with a second horse. You'll have time on your hands, with Vanessa so much occupied with

Justin, won't you?'

Amanda gave him a wary look. She had an instinctive feeling that it was not just a simple, friendly offer, that something else lay beneath it. Was Randall trying to spite his brother? Or to start a holiday flirtation with her? No, she decided, it was meant as an offer of alliance. Randall did not get on with Justin, and guessed she did not like him, either. So let's get together, he seemed to be saying. 'It's a kind offer, but I won't be short of occupation,' she answered. 'I intend to do some studying, and my parents are going away for a holiday soon. Vanessa and I will be doing the housekeeping while they're away.'

'Well, you can let me know later, if you'd like it,' said Randall lightly. He remounted his horse, and Amanda returned to her car, but sat for a few more minutes watching them.

When Vanessa came home, later in the evening, her hand was adorned by a beautiful sapphire and diamond engagement ring. 'It's a family heirloom,' she said proudly. 'Justin's had it altered to fit, and I'd much rather have it than any new ring.'

Amanda admired the ring sincerely enough to please Vanessa, but wondered again if Vanessa was in love with Justin, or only with this sort of glamour, of family and pedigree, things she was quite unused to. She did look the picture of a girl happily in love, but Vanessa was a bit of a chameleon, apt to take her colour from her surroundings or companions, whereas Amanda always remained obstinately the same.

'I've asked Justin to come to dinner one evening, while the parents are away,' Vanessa told her. 'You won't mind?'

'No; except that two's company, and three's none. I could go over to the farm, and leave you to yourselves, if you'd rather.'

'Oh, no. I want you to get to know Justin. And I don't want to do all the cooking.'

'I see,' laughed Amanda. 'I'm no better cook than you, but you can put the blame on me, if anything goes wrong. I wouldn't mind.'

'I could ask one of the others, and make it a foursome. Would you like me to ask Randall, or Caroline?'

'Not Caroline. I didn't care for her at all. Ask Randall, if you want to, but it doesn't matter to me.'

The wonderful holiday they had planned, when Vanessa first inherited her money, seemed to have gone for good. Last summer, they had been too busy moving, so had postponed it. When Amanda had mentioned it earlier this summer Vanessa had hedged, for reasons that now seemed obvious. Amanda was only mildly regretful. She was always happy in Northumberland, loved walking in the hills, and did not in the least mind doing it alone.

Two mornings later, they saw their parents off on holiday, then did a round of shopping. Vanessa was spending the afternoon with Justin. Amanda had intended to study, but decided it was too good a day to be spent indoors, she would go for a walk. She only got as far as the cross-roads, five minutes from the cottage. There she met Randall, riding one horse, and leading another. 'I was coming to your house,' he greeted her. 'Knowing Vanessa would be out, I thought you might like a ride with me. Are you going somewhere special, or will you join me?'

'I'm not dressed for riding,' Amanda hesitated.

'But you're only five minutes from home. How long would it take you to change that skirt for pants? When I've taken the trouble to bring a horse, you won't refuse, surely? Look at her, she's a beauty.'

'She is, indeed. Well, if you don't mind waiting,' agreed Amanda.

Randall walked to the cottage with her, and in a very short time, she was out again. She'd hesitated only because she felt that to refuse a horse from Justin, and then accept it from Randall, might seem a bit rude. But to refuse to go with Randall would have been even more uncivil, and it was a perfect day for riding; sunny, with an exhilarating wind.

They rode a little way along the road, then left it for a moorland track. Amanda found the mare, Bronwen, a sheer delight to ride, and Randall seemed to know all the hill tracks. He took her by ways that were known to her, and some that were new. Hills rippled gently away into the distance, and the wind blew with a freshness unknown in tree-clad country. Soon, Amanda's cheeks were flushed, and her hair blown into untidy ends by the breeze. They kept mostly to hill tracks, but still had to cross a few roads. Approaching one, Randall, who was in the lead, suddenly chuckled, and exclaimed softly: 'Just look who's here!'

Drawing level with him, Amanda was just in time to see a car slow to a halt. Justin was driving, Vanessa beside him. The top was down, to let in the sunshine, so it was easy for her to see that Vanessa was furious. What Justin thought was impossible to say, as he surveyed them with cool, grey eyes. Randall grinned widely: 'Don't you think Amanda looks well on Bronwen, Justin? She's a grand rider, and doesn't jib at borrowing a horse from *me*.'

Amanda had been embarrassed enough by this unlucky encounter, but Randall's mocking remark completed her confusion. She couldn't have spoken if she had tried. She saw Justin's mouth harden, but he answered, still very coolly: 'Enjoy yourselves.' The only sign that he was angry was the abruptness with which the car shot forward.

As soon as they were over the road, Amanda turned to Randall, and saw his eyes alight with mischief and satisfaction. 'That was unfair,' she exclaimed indignantly. 'If you want to score off your brother, that's your affair, but you'd no right to drag me into it.'

'I merely stated a plain fact,' he retorted. 'You refused the loan of a horse from Justin, and then accepted it from me. You don't like Justin, so why fuss about his feelings?'

'Because I do care about Vanessa, and I know she'll be furious with me for seeming rude to Justin.'

'Oh, well, I'm sorry,' said Randall, not very contritely. 'But if you had to live with Justin, I bet you couldn't resist any chance to score. You've no idea what he's like. He wants to be absolute ruler in everything, even down to criticizing the grocery bills! I know he's managing the estate, but it's not his yet. As long as it belongs to Father, he should run it as Father wishes, not just to suit himself. He's even had the nerve to sell one of our cars, so three of us have to use one car, turn about, while he keeps one entirely for his own use. But he'll never persuade Father to sell the horses, and it riles him to know I've as good a right to ride them as he has.'

The pent-up bitterness of Randall's voice startled Amanda. She had already guessed that the two brothers did not get on, but the depth of Randall's resentment did surprise her. Curiosity made her wish he would say more, but he did not, and she would not ask. When they reached the cross-roads, she stopped, and Randall looked at her with the mischief back in his eyes again. 'Well, will you come riding with me again?'

'I don't know.'

'But you enjoyed it.'

'Very much. Well, perhaps; I'll see,' Amanda dismounted, said good-bye, and walked the short distance to the cottage, wondering if Vanessa had reached home before her.

Vanessa was back, and flew at her in a fury. 'Amanda, how could you? To turn down Justin's offer of a horse, almost rudely, and then accept one from Randall, only a few days later! It was a deliberate insult to Justin.'

'I know it looked bad,' Amanda admitted, 'but how was I to know we'd meet? I didn't *plan* it. I started out for a walk, and then met Randall at the cross-roads. Knowing you were out, he thought I might like a ride, and had brought a second horse. I didn't see how I could refuse, without being rude to *him*. And how could I have stopped Randall being rude to his own brother?'

'Oh!' said Vanessa, considerably deflated. 'All the same, it was insulting to take a favour from Randall, just after refusing it from Justin.'

Amanda looked thoughtfully at her sister's angry face. Vanessa had quite a quick temper, but it was not easily roused. Did the present storm mean that she really was in love with Justin, and hated to see him slighted? Or had he, perhaps, made her suffer for that unlucky encounter? 'Was Justin angry?' she asked.

'He didn't say anything,' answered Vanessa, rather shortly.

'H'm; silence can sometimes be felt more than any words. Well, I'm sorry, but I think you're making a mountain out of a molehill, and I can't feel I was much to blame. You wanted me to be friendly with the Warrens, so I didn't feel that I could be unfriendly to Randall.'

'You don't know him as well as I do,' retorted Vanessa. 'He's madly jealous of Justin, because he's the eldest, and will inherit Danesford; and because Randall made a bid for me, before Justin came up here. His motives were pretty obvious, and I soon discouraged him, but now he'd love to make mischief between Justin and me. He was simply using you.'

'You're probably right. I must say the Warrens sound a delightful family. Would you have wanted me to be unfriendly to Randall, particularly when he's coming here for dinner tomorrow?'

'No, of course not,' Vanessa admitted. 'It was awkward for you; but if you'd accepted Justin's original offer, none of this would have arisen. Oh, well, let's forget it.'

Amanda was only too ready to do so. She disliked Randall's manner to his brother, but less than she might have done, if she had liked that brother a little more.

Vanessa was anxious that everything should go well, when Justin and

Randall came to dinner. She left Amanda to plan the meal, but they shared the work equally. Amanda did not expect much pleasure from the evening, especially after yesterday's encounter, but it would give her an opportunity to see Justin and Vanessa together, and perhaps get some clearer idea about their feelings for each other. Vanessa was over-anxious and fussed about the dinner, which might indicate love, or merely that Justin was hard to please, and she knew it.

Amanda remained annoyingly placid and unconcerned. She had planned a meal that could be prepared in advance, and was easy to serve; melon and fruit juice; then a chicken casserole, with tomatoes and green peppers, attractive to look at, and needing no carving. They would finish with a creamy peach sweet, and she was just finishing this off when Vanessa came into the kitchen. She wore a new dress of blues and greens, her hair in a soft dark cloud around her shoulders, and paused in the doorway. 'M'm,' said Amanda, appreciatively, 'that should knock him.'

Vanessa laughed, pleased by her praise, but instantly became anxious again. 'Amanda, do go and get ready. They may be here in ten minutes, and you don't want Justin to see you like that, do you?'

'Why should he bother to look at me, when he can look at you? All right, all right, look at my handsome sweet, and then I'll go.'

She ran upstairs, and made a very rapid toilet. Neither of their visitors was likely to care how she looked. Randall was only interested in her as a possible ally in his vendetta against his brother, and Justin was not interested in her at all. Amanda was a little affronted by this, not on her own account, but on Vanessa's. Anyone who really loved Vanessa would surely be interested in her sister, and want her to think well of him. Though Amanda did not like Justin, she was extremely interested in him, his character, his personality, and his motives for marrying Vanessa.

She ran downstairs, and paused for Vanessa's inspection and approval. Vanessa was the prettier of the two, her pale, creamy skin contrasting dramatically with her black hair, and vividly blue eyes; but Amanda did not suffer from the comparison, because she was very much the livelier. She had a natural grace and gaiety of movement, a glow of life in her whole body, and her simple green dress accentuated the auburn lights in her brown hair, and the bright warmth of her hazel eyes. She made a rapid inspection of pans and casseroles, and then the door-bell rang. 'You go, while I dish up,' she told Vanessa.

A couple of minutes later, Randall poked his head round the kitchen door. 'Can I help?'

'Everything's ready, but perhaps you'd carry in this tray. I hope everything will be all right.'

'We've both got good digestions,' said

Randall, with a grin.

'That's reassuring,' Amanda laughed back. 'I don't think they'll be taxed, but I'm afraid I was thinking more of Vanessa than of you. She'll be upset, if anything goes wrong.'

They went into the dining-room together, carrying the first course. Amanda had resolved to forget the previous day's unpleasantness, and be her friendliest to both their guests. But her smile dimmed a little, when she met Justin's reserved grey eyes. With all his faults, Randall was open and frank, but Justin's face was so unexpressive that it was impossible ever to guess what he was thinking. They exchanged surface-friendly greetings, but the atmosphere was somewhat stiff. They were too carefully on their best behaviour, so that an appearance of friendliness was preserved, but naturalness and spontaneity sacrificed.

Everything was perfectly cooked, and as Vanessa relaxed the atmosphere began to thaw. She and Randall both had long tongues, and knew each other well. Amanda had less to say than usual, but used her eyes and ears instead. She looked from Vanessa's flushed cheeks and eyes bright with pleasure, to Justin's too impassive face. What sort of man was he, beneath that massive reserve? Did he love Vanessa; or merely think she would make just the wife he required, decorative, easily guided, and with a comfortable fortune?

Justin glanced round, their eyes met, and a flicker of amusement showed in his. Amanda flushed, annoyed with herself for showing her thoughts too clearly, and with him for reading them so easily. She turned determinedly towards Randall, and began to talk to him. When she paused, he asked: 'When will you come riding with me again? Father says you're welcome to any of *his* horses, any time you like.'

There was a meaningful emphasis on the pronoun, and a look of devilment in his blue eyes. Justin and Vanessa had fallen silent, and were obviously meant to hear the remark. Amanda was uncomfortably aware of unpleasant undercurrents in the atmosphere. She answered very carefully. 'Not for the time being, though I enjoyed it. I planned to do a good deal of studying, and have done none yet.'

'Don't let me put you off,' said Justin. 'The horses could do with more exercise than they get.'

His bland, formal politeness was about as unexpressive as his face. 'You're both very kind,' said Amanda, equally polite, 'but it's more than time I did a bit of work.'

'What subjects are you taking?' enquired Justin, firmly moving on to neutral conversational ground. After that, the meal continued smoothly enough, but without much life. Amanda was so anxious not to offend Vanessa again that she was much less at ease than usual, and afraid of being drawn once more into the smouldering differences of the Warren brothers.

They had decided to leave the

washing-up until next day, but when Randall offered to help, Amanda agreed, thinking that everyone might be happier if they split up for a while. She and Randall washed up, and fed the animals, not hurrying themselves at all. When they re-joined the others, the cat and poodle went with them, and brought a little extra life into the party. But Amanda still felt a good deal of relief when their visitors left.

Vanessa went to the gate to see them off. She returned, looking put out. 'The evening was a flop, and it was your fault,' she told Amanda.

'My fault!' Amanda was both astonished and indignant. 'There's gratitude! They were your visitors, but I did more than half the cooking, and all the washing-up, and was *very* careful to say nothing wrong.'

'We'd agreed to leave the washing-up; and then you decided to do it, and stayed out for ages and ages.'

'We thought we were being tactful,' said Amanda, with an irrepressible grin.

'Engaged couples usually like some time to themselves.'

'You stayed in the kitchen because you disliked being agreeable to Justin. You had practically nothing to say to him, but you were laughing and talking with Randall the whole time you were in the kitchen.'

'Randall's easy to talk to,' said Amanda slowly. 'Justin's so reserved. I don't know what interests him, but I have tried to like him.'

'I don't think you've tried very hard.'

'Don't you think it's expecting too much, Vanessa, to think I *must* like Justin, because you do? You don't like all my friends. Remember Betty Taylor.'

'She was dreadfully common.'

This was such an echo of her mother's snobbery that it grated on Amanda. 'You mean her manners were a bit different from ours,' she flashed. 'But Mrs Warren and Caroline probably think us dreadfully common, and swallow us only because of your money.'

'And I suppose the real meaning of

that is that Justin must be marrying me for my money,' exclaimed Vanessa, furiously.

'We weren't talking about Justin. And if we were, surely it's natural for me to want to feel quite sure your money has nothing to do with it?'

'Why do you take it for granted that I'm incapable of thinking for myself?'

Amanda let this pass, and said in a conversational tone: 'Richard's still in love with you.'

That Vanessa was startled by this sudden change of subject was shown in the betraying stillness of her face, and a certain tautness of voice. 'He was never in love with me, nor I with him.'

'He asked all sorts of questions, and would have listened to me talking about you for a whole evening. But you haven't asked a single question about him. Doesn't old friendship mean anything to you?'

Vanessa flushed right up to the roots of her hair. 'Anne sometimes writes, and gives me any news,' she said defensively. 'I'm tired. You can stay up, if you want, but I'm going,' and getting to her feet she departed with unusual rapidity.

Amanda sat on, thoughtful and puzzled. She agreed with Vanessa, that the evening had been less than a success, but did not think it was her fault. She had made an effort to like Justin, but he did not seem at all anxious to be liked. Why should he present such an impenetrable wall of reserve, unless he knew that his motives for marrying Vanessa would not bear examination?

Vanessa had been angry, and almost on the verge of tears, because of the failure of the evening. That suggested that Justin was very important to her. But Amanda remained convinced that she was not as indifferent to Richard as she made out. That swift departure for bed had all the air of a retreat. Amanda still felt that she would not have told Anne of her engagement, before telling her, unless she had been very anxious that Richard should know it at the first possible moment. Why should that matter, if she really was indifferent to him? And yet, on the other hand, she had asked nothing about him. Vanessa looked perfectly happy, but in the days of her friendship with Richard, she had had a light-hearted gaiety, which Amanda missed now. She sighed, and felt baffled; resolved to have another go at trying to understand and like Justin, and followed Vanessa to bed.

3

The next morning the fine weather broke. Vanessa was out most of the day, accompanying Justin to the local town, where he had business. Amanda did some concentrated studying. After a day apart, they were both ready to forget yesterday's differences. Vanessa recounted the small events of her day, adding: 'Justin wants to take us out to dinner, sometime. They can't do any entertaining at Danesford, while his father is so unwell.'

'Does "us" mean yesterday's foursome?' asked Amanda. 'It didn't exactly go with a swing, did it?'

Vanessa looked at the rueful amusement in her eyes, and gave a reluctant grin. 'Not exactly. Would you rather leave Randall out?'

'Not if it means my making a third with you and Justin.' Amanda thought for a moment, then suggested: 'You could ask my cousin Frank. As he's in farming, he and Justin should have plenty to talk about.'

'That's a good idea,' agreed Vanessa. 'I'm taking Justin over to Hesket some day, so we could fix something up with Frank then.'

They had two more days of drenching rain. On the fourth day, it began to clear around midday. Vanessa was out with Justin. Amanda, tired of indoors and books, decided to chance more showers and go for a walk. But she had not even reached the cross-roads when the rain came pelting down again. She dived for the shelter of some trees, and struggled into her mac. A car came round the corner, and braked to a halt beside her. Looking up, she saw Randall Warren and his sister. Leaning across Caroline, Randall asked: 'What are you doing there?'

'Sheltering, of course. And wondering whether to go on, or go home.'

'Don't do either. Come with us. We're sick of the house, and decided to go over to the coast. Sometimes it's dryer there, and at least it's dry inside the car. Do join us.'

Amanda hesitated, then accepted, not so much because she wanted the drive, or their company, as from interest in the Warren family, and Justin in particular. And it would be a change from her books. Randall talked most of the time, about anything and nothing, as he drove, but Caroline had little to say. It was still raining when they reached the coast. Randall stopped on an almost deserted prom, and they sat watching the rain falling across the sea, and the sun struggling to come out from between the clouds. 'How are you getting on with training Thunder?' Amanda asked.

Randall grinned ruefully. 'I can get him across the water nine times out of ten, now; but the tenth time he still jibs. I shall ride him at Thurston, and hope for the best.' He went on talking horses. Caroline looked bored, but not Amanda. She liked horses, and was not easily bored. 'I wanted to make horses my job, when I was a kid,' he told her. 'Breeding and training them, and riding too, of course. But it needs too much money, to do it well.'

'What are you planning to do now?' she asked.

'I've just completed a course in estate management.'

Amanda considered this in silence. It seemed a curious, not to say tactless course to have chosen, as Randall could only inherit the family estate if his brother died. Perhaps sensing her thoughts, Caroline came suddenly to life. 'Father wanted Randall to take that course. Running the estate was becoming rather a burden to him, so he wanted him to take on some of it. Of course Danesford will be Justin's, some day, but that day seemed pretty distant before Father's heart attack. He wanted Randall to help him with the estate for a couple of years, get experience, and then perhaps take over the tenancy of one of the farms. But his illness changed everything. Someone had to manage the estate. Randall hadn't finished his training, so Justin was the obvious person. Things were a bit difficult financially, and he's an expert in agricultural economics. Unfortunately, he's altogether too much of an economist.'

'You've said it!' Randall groaned.

'You go about things the wrong way,' said Caroline dispassionately. 'You will tackle Justin head-on, and then you both lose your tempers.'

'But he can't block everything *you* want, as he does with me. Ridley's Farm falls vacant in October. As Justin won't allow me any share in running the estate, Father promised I should have the farm. Now, Justin says no, I can't have that, either. He's no right to over-rule Father, but he acts as though the place belongs to him already.'

'But can he?' asked Amanda, rather shocked by these revelations. 'Has he the power to stop your father giving you the farm?'

'He can't prevent Father's giving me the tenancy, but what's the good of a farm, and no money for stock and machinery? And Justin can sit tight on the money-bags. Father planned to sell some timber, to give me a start, but he has to have Justin's agreement, and Justin won't give it. I'm handicapped, because it's bad for Father to be worried. I daren't involve him in a real battle with Justin.'

'Justin says that the trees must not be felled for another five to ten years,' explained Caroline, in her cool voice. 'They'll be worth more then, apart from the possibility that they may be Justin's trees, by then. He won't agree to the estate's being impoverished in the very smallest way, not even to give Randall a decent start.'

Amanda was deeply shocked by these candid revelations of a family rent by internal differences, shocked equally by the nature of the differences, and that they should be revealed so frankly to an outsider. But she was undeniably fascinated. She wanted to learn all she could about the man Vanessa intended to marry. She would not ask prying questions, but she could not resist listening.

'Rowing with Justin will get you nowhere,' Caroline told her brother. 'He's got the whip hand now, and intends to use it. Next year, Father may be well enough to take charge of his own affairs again, and then he'll give you the farm, or the management of the estate. In the meantime, you've got a good diploma, and should get a job in another part of the country. Or you could have a third year in college.'

'Oh, no; I'm not going to take myself conveniently out of the way,' retorted Randall grimly. 'And for why? because I know Justin's got his eye on Ridley's, for himself. He wouldn't need money from the estate to farm it. Not with a rich wife!'

There was a sudden silence. Amanda looked at the two faces before her, Randall's flushed and resentful, Caroline's wearing a kind of resigned amusement, and wondered why they were being so very out-spoken. Perhaps it was just their nature. Perhaps they wanted her to warn Vanessa that she was being married for her money. Or was it calculated spite, inspired by the hope that she could persuade Vanessa to break her engagement to Justin? Not this last, Amanda decided. It was all too casual, too premeditated, and Randall was too angry to weigh his words. He might be exaggerating, but she could not doubt his sincerity.

'Justin could run the estate and the farm together,' Randall went on. 'Later, if Father's well enough to manage the estate, Justin could run the farm as a full time job; or get a job in one of the northern universities, and keep the farm as a side-line. Either way, he'd have a permanent observation post, from which he could interfere in everything. And he would. Cash always comes first with Justin. But Father listens to me too, so I intend to stick around, and see that Justin doesn't grab everything for himself.'

'You looked shocked.' Caroline surveyed Amanda with amusement. 'You think we shouldn't speak of a brother like this. But Justin's never been quite one of us. Maybe that shocks you too, but we didn't make him an outsider. Justin's always been a loner. He lived with Grandfather, after his mother died, and was very thoroughly spoilt. She was killed in a car smash. Father was quite badly hurt too, and after he came out of hospital, he shut up his house and went abroad, leaving Justin at Danesford. After that, he travelled a good deal, and never really settled down, until he married again. Mother found Justin very difficult. He used to run away, back to his grandfather, every time he couldn't get his own way, and he's always kept himself a little apart from the rest of us. He's terribly possessive, and would never allow us to lay a finger on anything of his. Of course younger kids can be a nuisance, but he kept all his books and all his toys in his bedroom, and wouldn't allow us into it. When he went to school, he had a lock put on his cupboard, locked everything in it, and took the key to school with him.'

For some reason, this small detail shocked Amanda more than anything that had gone before. It seemed oddly revealing, and confirmed her darkest suspicions about Justin's engagement to Vanessa.

'It's easy for you to treat it lightly,' Randall told his sister. 'You don't intend to stay and put up with things. You'll follow Justin's example, and marry someone with plenty of money.'

'Certainly,' agreed Caroline composedly. 'Life's not going to be much fun at Danesford, with Justin's passion for small economies. But there are several applicants, and I haven't decided which will suit me best.'

She criticized Justin, yet she was remarkably like him, thought Amanda. She had the same aloof self-sufficiency, always looked cool, immaculate, and very sure of herself. She was a little younger than Amanda, but seemed much older. Randall, though a year older, seemed a mere boy beside Caroline. Amanda liked him the best of the Warrens. With all his faults, he was friendly and natural, and much more human than Caroline and Justin.

'Let's go and have some tea,' he said, and drove them to the best hotel in the place. The young Warrens seemed to feel no need to count the pennies. When they came out again, the rain was off, so they went for a walk along the prom, before returning to the car. Then Randall discovered he was out of cigarettes, and went off to buy some.

'Poor Randall, he really is miserable,' said Caroline, and for the first time there was some real warmth in her voice. Amanda realized that, in her own way, she was fond of Randall. 'The truth is, he and Justin both want Danesford, but only one of them can have it. And they've both been spoilt; Justin by Grandfather, and Randall by Father. Randall's always been Father's favourite. He'd like to leave Danesford to him, but it's entailed, so there it is. And things aren't made easier by Justin's possessiveness. *Danesford will be mine, not yours*, he was continually telling Randall, when we were children. He doesn't put it quite so crudely now, but the sentiment's still the same. And now he's going to marry Vanessa, and it does seem as though Justin gets everything, and Randall nothing.'

Not Vanessa, if I can help it, thought Amanda. She said nothing, but she had a very expressive face. Caroline looked amused again. 'Oh, well, I expect Vanessa knows what she's doing. Danesford's a very fine place, and Justin will see that the estate pays good dividends, once it's his. Already, he plans everything for *future* profit, at the expense of present enjoyment.'

Randall returned, and drove them back. When he stopped at the cottage, he said: 'I think the weather's going to pick up. Will you come for a ride with me tomorrow, if it does?'

'I'd like to,' Amanda answered. Let Justin think whatever he liked!

Vanessa was in before her. She listened to Amanda's account of where she had been, then embarked on her own. 'I took Justin to Hesket this afternoon. He and Grandfather got on very well together. We went over to the farmhouse afterwards, and fixed up to take you and Frank out to dinner, tomorrow evening.'

'Oh!' said Amanda. She felt in no mood for a whole evening of trying to be friendly to Justin. 'That will be nice,' she added politely.

She was not simple-minded enough to accept unquestioningly everything Caroline and Randall had said about their brother. They obviously did not get on with him, and resented his disruption of their pleasant existence. But none of their criticisms seemed contrary to Justin's personality, so far as Amanda could guess at it. Randall and Caroline had agreed on every material point. Justin's extreme regard for money, his possessiveness, his determination that Randall should have nothing from the estate, and they seemed to take it completely for granted that he was marrying Vanessa for her money. Caroline obviously saw nothing wrong in that. She and Justin were two of a kind, thought Amanda disgustedly, the same cold practicality and self-sufficiency. But Vanessa was not like that. She would never calculate, in Caroline's cold-blooded fashion, that Danesford, and the prestige of becoming a Warren, were a fair exchange for her fortune. She might be genuinely in love with Justin; or she might be living in an unreal dream of a glamorous future. In either case, Amanda was afraid that she might have a bitter awakening, unless her eyes could be opened in time.

Amanda spent a pleasant afternoon riding in the hills with Randall, returning home only just in time to get ready for their evening with Justin. Vanessa had another new dress for the occasion, white with a black frill. It made her look older, more sophisticated. But Amanda wore the green dress she had worn for their own unsuccessful dinner. She liked it, and knew Frank too well, and disliked Justin too much to fuss over clothes. Frank arrived first, Justin very soon afterwards, interrupting a pleasant, cousinly gossip. He drove them about twenty miles, to a country inn, where the food was excellent.

Justin and Frank did most of the talking during the meal, mainly about farming matters. Amanda, a farmer's granddaughter, knew far more about the subject than Vanessa, and became interested, almost in spite of herself. She was honest enough to admit that Justin never tried to condescend to a younger, less experienced man. He asked questions, and listened intently to Frank's answers, but he harped far too much on the cash aspect of farming. His most constantly repeated query was — can you make it show a profit?

Amanda learnt that Justin was at present managing the home farm, as well as the estate. Speaking of this, he went on to say: 'Another farm, Ridley's, will be vacant in October. I'd rather not let it again. It would make a much more profitable unit, if it could be amalgamated with the home farm. But that would require more capital than is available, at the moment.'

Amanda was reminded of Randall's disclosures. Ridley's was the farm that had been promised to him, by his father, which he said Justin had his eye on, for himself. This remark seemed to confirm his surmise, and she could easily guess whose money Justin was hoping to use, later on, to further his plans. She became even more silent, her thoughts written a little too plainly on her face.

In the midst of a discussion about corn, Frank turned to her, saying: 'If you want to be a plant-breeder, Amanda, maybe you know more about it than us.'

Justin glanced at her with quick interest: 'Is that what you're planning to do?'

'It's what I'd like to do, but openings are rather limited,' answered Amanda, her voice unconsciously cool, and very discouraging.

Justin's eyes lingered on her face for a few moments, then with an invisible mental shrug, he returned to his conversation with Frank. Amanda felt suddenly ashamed of herself, guessing what Vanessa would be thinking. She had not meant to sound so snubbing, but the truth was that she was no good at concealing her thoughts and feelings, unlike Vanessa, who could act a part well enough to deceive her nearest and dearest, perhaps even herself. And now Vanessa might accuse her of spoiling this party, too. Amanda took a grip on herself, and tried to make a livelier fourth.

When they got back, Frank refused to come in, saying he had to make a very early start next day. Justin also excused himself, so Amanda said good-bye to them both, and went indoors, leaving Vanessa to say good-bye to Justin alone. When she followed Amanda inside, she asked: 'Why did you bother to come, if you intended to cast a blight on the whole evening?'

Amanda knew there was some truth in this accusation. If she had not gone out with Randall and Caroline, it might have been a more enjoyable evening for everyone. 'I didn't *mean* to be a blight,' she answered, but that sounded lame, even to herself.

'What have you got against Justin?' demanded Vanessa. 'You hardly know him.'

There were several answers Amanda could have made, none that she really wanted to make. If she repeated her conversation with Randall and Caroline, Vanessa would accuse her of lending a ready ear to malicious gossip. Some of it might have been malicious, though Justin had confirmed one item, that very evening. 'We just seem to be like oil and water,' she said slowly. 'We don't mix.'

'Well, at least, Justin's always good-mannered, and that's more than I'd say for you,' retorted Vanessa, acidly. 'What

80

did Randall and Caroline say about him yesterday? You should know better than to listen to them. I've told you Randall's madly jealous of Justin. Oh, well, if you won't behave reasonably to him, I'll just have to keep you apart.'

She departed to bed, shutting the door very forcibly behind her. Amanda sat down, with the cat on her knee, feeling both guilty and unhappy. She and Vanessa had always been such very good friends, and now Justin seemed to be driving a wedge between them. She knew this was partly her own fault, that she had behaved somewhat childishly this evening, but only because she was so fond of Vanessa. She didn't think she could ever feel much warmth of liking for Justin, but if she could only feel that Vanessa loved him and that he had no ulterior motive for marrying her, then she would find it easy to tolerate him, and behave in a much friendlier fashion.

By morning, Vanessa had recovered her usual good-humour. The two girls got on well together in the house, and by tacit consent, went their separate ways outside it. Vanessa spent a lot of time with Justin, and Amanda was left very much to her own resources, but did not mind in the least. She could be happy almost anywhere, and nowhere so easily as in her native Northumberland. She loved walking among the moorland heights and lonely glens through which ran the border of Scotland and England; finding a pleasant place where she could linger, enjoying the wide silence, space and serenity, the faint wild fragrance on the breeze, which spoke to her of home as only scents can speak.

Nearly a week after that dinner with Justin, she came home in the early evening, loitering, because she had walked a good few rough miles that day. She climbed over a stile, and had begun to descend a rough, tussocky field when the gate at the bottom swung open, and Justin came through. Amanda's feet slowed involuntarily, but the path went straight downhill to the gate. Unless she retreated, she could not avoid meeting him.

Justin turned from fastening the gate, and saw her. He hesitated, just long enough for Amanda to guess that he relished this unavoidable meeting as little as she did. Then he came slowly up the path. 'I thought you were driving with Vanessa,' Amanda remarked, trying to make her voice sound friendly.

'I took her home an hour ago. She hasn't your liking for hill walks.' Amanda glanced at him, wondering why he was walking alone in the hills. As though reading the question in her eyes, he added: 'I'm here in the way of work. This is a part of the estate.'

'Oh! I didn't know this was Warren land.'

'Or you'd have taken another path, to avoid soiling your feet?' suggested Justin, an unmistakably sardonic glint in his eyes.

Amanda had made a real effort to be friendly, and felt that it had been flung back in her face. Her cheeks flushed to a stormy brightness. 'It is a right of way, isn't it?' she asked stiffly.

'Of course. This is part of Ridley's Farm. We were talking about it the other evening.'

If Amanda had been less angry, she might have seen that Justin regretted that sarcastic thrust, and wanted to make amends, but she noticed only the name of the farm. 'The farm your father promised to Randall,' she said thoughtlessly.

There was a silence, lasting long enough for Amanda to wish she could take that remark back. Justin's face hardened and closed. 'So, Randall airs family disagreements to all and sundry.'

'Oh, no, I'm sure he doesn't.' Amanda rushed to defend Randall, and herself. 'I asked him what he was planning to do, for a career. He said he didn't know, because his plan to farm here had been upset.'

'And, of course, you were very ready to believe anything to my disadvantage.

Don't you know there are two sides to every question?'

If Justin had been angry, Amanda would have liked him better, but he remained provokingly calm and superior. 'Of course I do, but one side may be a lot better than the other. Is it true that your father promised this farm to Randall?'

'Quite true.'

There was a grim look about Justin's mouth, and Amanda hesitated before asking: 'And you've made it impossible for him to keep that promise?'

'True again,' he answered with cool deliberation. 'Randall is a spendthrift and irresponsible, and I refuse to back his fantastic claims. I suppose that makes me a monster?'

'No, but a pretty fair dog-in-the-manger,' she answered, with scornful honesty.

'Well, for your further information, I am here to make a final inspection before deciding whether to let the farm, or take it myself. It's so run-down, it might be difficult to get a good tenant, so I've decided to farm it myself, and give it a complete modernization.'

His cool grey eyes rested on Amanda's flushed face, aware of her antagonism, and apparently quite indifferent to it. 'Vanessa's money should come in very handy for that,' she remarked, with reckless candour; and had the brief satisfaction of seeing that, for once, she had got under Justin's guard. His eyes flinched away from hers, and he swung abruptly away, down the field.

Amanda watched him go, her anger cooling as quickly as it had flared up, and wishing she had stopped to think, before she let her tongue run away with her. Justin had admitted the truth of Randall's accusation, and even seemed to boast of what he had done. She had not the slightest wish to be friends with him. The trouble was that she wanted to remain friends with Vanessa, and Vanessa would be very angry indeed, if Justin repeated their conversation.

Amanda walked on down the path, pondering this. Justin might repeat her remarks, just to make trouble for her, but then he would have to admit that he had forced his father to break a promise. And she was reasonably sure he would not repeat her final words. Justin did not seem to care what she thought of his dealings with Randall, but he had not liked that reference to Vanessa's money. There was too much truth in it for his comfort, thought Amanda, more than ever convinced that Justin was marrying Vanessa only for her money. But Vanessa would not heed anything she said on that score. Vanessa thought she was hopelessly, unreasonably prejudiced against Justin. Amanda felt miserably helpless, and said nothing to her sister about that chance meeting.

She knew Vanessa was going out with Justin the next day. When she returned, quite unruffled, she decided that Justin had also chosen to keep quiet about their encounter. Vanessa told her she would be out for the whole of the following day. Justin was taking her to Thurston Show. 'We could have gone together, if only you'd be a bit more friendly,' she complained. 'There would be room, if you'd like to come.'

'I'd like to see Randall ride, but a whole day with Justin, no, that would be too risky,' answered Amanda, and could not help wondering how Justin would have reacted to that prospect.

Soon after Vanessa had left, Amanda's cousin Frank rang up. Their grand-parents had decided to go to the Show, he told her, and they'd like her to join them. Amanda agreed with enthusiasm. In this safe company, she would thoroughly enjoy the Show. When they arrived there, Amanda and her grand-father, leaving Frank to escort his grandmother, went to potter amongst the farm machinery, and then to watch the horse-riding, horses being another interest they shared. They met again for lunch, then back to the horses for Amanda and her grandfather. She had the pleasure of watching Randall, on Thunder, come second in the jumping event, the horse taking the water jump without hesitation.

Soon after this, Mr Deane decided he'd had enough. While they were looking for the other two, they came face to face with Justin and Vanessa. Vanessa exclaimed in surprise; Amanda explained, and then cast a wary glance at Justin. He gave her a polite smile, which did not reach his eyes. Mr Deane praised Randall's riding, and Amanda listened while they talked horses, then thankfully caught sight of her grandmother. They exchanged good-byes, and parted, with relief on Amanda's side.

4

Three days after Thurston Show, Mr and Mrs Carr were due to return from their holiday. With two whole days in hand, the girls decided to give up the last one to a burst of shopping, cooking, and house-cleaning, and do just as they pleased with the other. As it was a day of bright, windy sunshine, Amanda packed a few sandwiches, and set off for a moorland walk.

She went by familiar paths, enjoying the wild, lonely beauty of the hills, and the small burns flowing clear and brown and cool. By the time she had finished her lunch, clouds were racing up from the west, and the wind was distinctly cooler. She decided to take a shorter route home, over the shoulder of a hill, and then downhill to a stream. She had to cross it by a row of stepping-stones, which stood clear of the water in dry weather. Today, they were half-submerged by rushing brown water. Unsurprised, Amanda sat down, and pulled off shoes and stockings. Tucking them under her arm, she stepped cautiously on to the first stone. It was covered by an inch of water, cold as ice. The temptation was strong to leap back to the bank, or scuttle across the stones as fast as she could. But Amanda had crossed those stones before, and knew that water-weeds clung to them, making them extremely slippery. She stepped slowly and carefully on to the second stone, then the third.

She was just poised for the fourth, when a movement to the left caught her eye. Turning her head, she saw Justin on horseback, still some distance away, but riding along the bank towards her. Instinctively, she quickened her steps, and that was her undoing. She stepped incautiously on to a weedy stone, her feet shot from beneath her, and she went splash into the river, flat on her back. It was not deep, but the suddenness and icy cold knocked the breath out of her for a moment. Then she scrambled to her feet, and waded over to the bank, ignoring the stepping-stones, being already as wet as she could be.

Justin had pushed his horse to a gallop. He jumped down, and reached out a hand to help her up the bank. Amanda would rather have ignored it, but it was steep on that side, so she accepted his help, and was pulled up on to the grassy bank. Justin looked down at her dripping, bedraggled form. He kept a grave face, but there was more than a suspicion of a grin about him, and Amanda felt an utter fool. 'I've crossed those stones dozens of times, and never fallen in before,' she said defensively. 'You startled me, appearing suddenly like that.'

'I'm sure it was entirely my fault,' he answered, though his eyes still twinkled suspiciously. 'But the most urgent question — '

He was interrupted by a yelp of

dismay from Amanda. 'My shoes! They were under my arm, and must have fallen in.'

'They're probably where you fell. I'll get them.'

'No, I will. I can't be wetter than I am.'

'But you could cut your feet.' Putting her firmly aside, he dropped down into the water. He found one shoe by the stepping-stones, but had to wade several yards downstream before finding the other, wedged between stones. Even in riding-boots, his feet would be soaked, thought Amanda. He scrambled up the bank, and held out the shoes. 'They're so soggy, I doubt if you'll be able to get your feet into them.'

'I shall have to. I can't go barefoot on stony paths.' Amanda sat down, and pushed and tugged until she had got her wet feet into even wetter shoes. By then, she was so cold that her teeth had begun to chatter.

'What you need is a hot bath, and dry clothes,' said Justin. 'Take my horse, and you'll be home in ten minutes.'

'Oh, I couldn't do that. How would you manage? I'll walk, and dry as I go.'

'And freeze as well. Up you get, and don't be silly.' Justin put out a long arm, and Amanda soon found herself in the saddle, only partly of her own free-will. 'I'm only going over to Eastwood Farm, and I'll walk home from there,' he added, gave the horse a pat on the rump, and told him to get going.

Looking back over her shoulder, Amanda called: 'I'll change into dry things, and then bring him back to you.'

'Nonsense! I'll walk, and collect him later.'

Amanda gave the horse his head. He was a lovely creature, easy-moving and swift, and they arrived at the cottage in a very short time. Amanda led the horse into the front garden, shut the gate behind him, and went indoors. Immediately, Vanessa popped out of the sitting-room. Her eyes widened, then she collapsed on to one of the lower stairs, and howled with laughter. 'I'm sure it's very funny,' said Amanda. 'But I'm sopping wet and cold, and you're blocking the stairs.'

'I'll run you a hot bath,' exclaimed Vanessa. 'But you'd laugh too, if only you could see yourself.' She ran upstairs, mopping her eyes as she went.

Amanda undressed in the bathroom, dropping her soaked garments on to the floor. 'Whatever have you been doing?' asked Vanessa.

'Falling into a river. I was crossing on some stepping-stones, and Justin came suddenly round a bend. I was so startled I fell in.'

'So I suppose it was all Justin's fault,' commented Vanessa, dryly.

'I did *not* say that. Much more mine. He kindly fished my shoes out of the river, and lent me his horse to get home.'

'Where's the horse now?'

'Shut in the front garden. He'll come to no harm there. I'll get into dry things, and then ride him back to the farm where Justin was going.'

'Don't be silly. It's going to rain. Have a good soak, and I'll get my car out, and fetch Justin. Where was he going?' Amanda told her. 'I'll bring him here for tea, and then he can take his horse home,' Vanessa added, and departed.

Amanda ran more hot water into the bath, and warmth seeped blissfully through her. Then Vanessa poked her head round the door. 'It *would* have to be Justin, wouldn't it?' she said sweetly, and vanished. Amanda glowered after her, but then her sense of humour, never long dormant, reasserted itself, and she began to laugh. Vanessa was right. The largest part of her annoyance was caused by the fact that it *would* have to be Justin. She freely admitted that he had behaved kindly and decisively, rescuing her shoes, and getting her home in quick time. But it was infuriating that she should have made a spectacle of herself before him.

She got out of the bath, dried, and

went to her room. She was somewhat casual and happy-go-lucky about clothes, as a rule, but thoughts of the bedraggled sight she had looked impelled her to wear her newest dress. It was very simple, but the autumn shades of brown, gold and bronze were just right with her bright chestnut hair, and smooth amber tan. It did something to restore her self-respect. She hung her wet garments in the wash-house. She'd have to wash them later. Then she investigated the larder. It was somewhat bare, as they intended to shop and bake next day, but she had assembled a passable tea, by the time Vanessa returned with Justin.

Amanda went to meet them. 'Goodness, your best dress!' exclaimed Vanessa, with total lack of tact. Then she giggled. 'You certainly *do* look different, doesn't she, Justin?'

'Very different, and very charming,' he answered, and Amanda sensed thinly veiled amusement behind his polite gravity.

She was not easily put out, but

Vanessa's tactless remark made her feel like a child who had dressed in her best, hoping to erase an unfortunate impression. She had gone to meet them, intending to thank Justin for his timely assistance, and to do her best to get on to friendlier terms with him. She turned silently back to the kitchen, feeling foolish. If Justin had not ridden by at just that moment, she thought, as she made the tea, she would have crossed the river without disaster, and finished her walk in peace. He had probably thoroughly enjoyed her discomfiture. He would hardly be human, if he had not.

Vanessa did most of the talking through tea, keeping up a lively and amusing flow. Their positions seemed to have been reversed since her engagement, thought Amanda. Vanessa had gained assurance, while she was perpetually being made to feel childish and silly. Was Vanessa's new confidence due to love? It was so difficult to be sure which was the *real* Vanessa, as distinct from the character she wanted to be at any given moment. And Justin's reserve made it equally difficult to know what he really thought and felt.

Before he left, Amanda made herself thank him for his help, but it was a slightly stilted little speech, very different from the spontaneous thanks she would have given him, when he first came in. When he had gone, Vanessa said: 'I heard a piece of news from Justin this morning. Caroline's engaged.'

'Really! I suppose the man has pots of money?'

Vanessa's cheeks flushed angrily. 'That's a pretty nasty remark! Why are you always getting at Justin?'

'As a matter of fact, I wasn't,' said Amanda patiently. 'Caroline stated, in my hearing, that life at Danesford was no longer to her taste, and she intended to get married, as soon as she had decided which candidate suited her best. As Caroline is an exceedingly practical young woman, I assumed that, other things being equal, she'd choose the man with the mostest. Has he got pots of money?'

'He's certainly not poor,' Vanessa answered reluctantly. 'His name's Jeremy Hartford. His family have an estate twenty miles from here, which they bought quite recently.'

'And I suppose Jeremy is the eldest son?' pressed Amanda; and Vanessa's reluctant grin was answer enough.

They spent the next day in a hectic scramble, getting everything ship-shape for their parents' return. The day after that, they went to meet them, and there was an enjoyable exchange of gossip, news, and presents. When Vanessa told her of Caroline's engagement, Mrs Carr asked as many questions as if Caroline had been a relation of her own. Listening to them, Amanda found herself wondering again, if Vanessa had been infected by her mother's snobbishness, her conviction that wealth and social position added enormously to anyone's worth as a human being. If, in fact, Vanessa had imagined herself in love with Justin, when she was only in love with a Warren of Danesford.

From talk of Caroline's engagement, Mrs Carr passed on to ask if Vanessa and Justin had decided when they were getting married. 'It's rather difficult,' said Vanessa. 'At first, Justin didn't think he'd stay up here, once his father was well enough to manage the estate again. But now, he's decided to rent one of the Danesford farms, and go on living here, whatever happens about the estate. But I don't like the farmhouse, and don't want to live there, if we can find anywhere better. And we can't decide on a date, until we've settled where we're going to live.'

Amanda was better pleased by this reply than Mrs Carr. She felt that any delay was good, because it would give Vanessa time for reflection. But she did wonder if Justin was equally willing to wait, or would rather be sure of his profitable alliance, as quickly as possible.

A few days later, Vanessa told her that

Mrs Warren was giving a dinner-party to celebrate Caroline's engagement. Because of Mr Warren's health, it would only be a small family party. Vanessa was invited, and so was Amanda. 'Me! Whatever for?' exclaimed Amanda, more dismayed than gratified. 'I'm not family. You didn't ask Mrs Warren to invite me, did you?'

'No, Randall did. Mrs Warren wanted an extra girl, to make the numbers even, and intended to ask some cousin. But Randall said he'd be stuck with her, and he'd rather have you; that you were a family connection, and more fun than his cousin. You will come?'

'I suppose so, but I've nothing to wear.'

'I'd like a new dress. We'll go shopping tomorrow, and I'll pay for yours. And don't go all independent. It's on my account you need the dress.'

'All right,' Amanda laughed. 'I'll accept, and say thank you kindly.'

They were still the best of friends, except when Justin's name cropped up.

Amanda let Vanessa choose both dresses, a pale golden yellow, the colour of Devonshire cream, for herself, and a soft jade green for Amanda.

Dressed for the party, Amanda inspected herself in the mirror. The jade green dress was exactly right with her colouring, brown hair with auburn lights, smooth even tan, and eyes that were neither green, brown nor grey, but a combination of all three. She went to Vanessa's room, and found her almost ready, looking lovely in her creamy-gold dress. 'You'll put Caroline in the shade,' said Amanda. 'I don't think I'll let you down, in appearance, at least.'

'I hope in nothing else,' exclaimed Vanessa.

'Oh, I promise to be on my very best behaviour.'

They were the last to arrive at Danesford. When they had been introduced to the Hartfords, parents and two sons, Randall provided Amanda with sherry. As she sipped it, her eyes went round the room, the old portraits on the walls, and masses of flowers everywhere. It looked so luxurious it seemed ridiculous to think the Warrens were hard-up. 'Penny for your thoughts,' said Randall, appearing suddenly beside her.

Amanda struggled between discretion and candour, and candour won, perhaps because Randall was so remarkably frank himself. 'This looks a very expensive party — those flowers alone! But you said Justin was terribly economical.'

'He's madly economical, but he's not giving this party,' said Randall, with wicked amusement. 'Mother's determined to do Caro proud, so she ordered regardless. There'll be a battle royal when the bills roll in, but it will be too late then.'

For the very first time Amanda felt an impulse of sympathy for Justin, having to cope with the extravagance of this family. All that display of florist's flowers, when they had a big garden!

Randall took her in to dinner, and she found herself placed between him and Mr Hartford. Randall's long tongue kept her entertained for some time, but then he turned to his other neighbour, and she found herself a little isolated. Her eyes went interestedly around the party. Caroline looked beautifully groomed, cool and poised, with none of the glow and sparkle Amanda thought proper for a newly engaged girl. Not that she expected that in Caroline. Her fiancé was on the short side, his skin rather pale beside the outdoor tan of Randall and Justin.

In his father's absence, Justin was at the head of the table, sitting under the portrait of one of his ancestors, and looking remarkably like him. And too much like his sister Caroline, thought Amanda, just the same cold, self-possessed indifference. He was not the right match for Vanessa, who was a warm-hearted, vulnerable girl, liable to batter and bruise herself against these cold, practical Warrens. Justin looked round at this moment, and caught Amanda's fixed gaze on him. His eyes changed to swift impatience, and she hastily looked away. She was glad when the party broke up. Before leaving, she agreed to ride with Randall, next day.

He arrived soon after lunch, bringing the brown mare, Bronwen, for her to ride. 'She's mine now, a birthday present from Father,' he told her. 'Rather belated, as my birthday was earlier, when he was ill. And now even birthday presents have to be vetted by Justin,' he added bitterly. 'But he couldn't stop Father making me a present of a couple of his own horses.'

Amanda found his confidences rather embarrassing, but soon forgot unpleasantness in the enjoyment of riding over wild, bendy hills, with a wind that smelt of heather and gorse. 'Come and look at my other new horse,' Randall suggested. 'I'd like you to see him, and you needn't go anywhere but the stables, if you don't want to.'

Amanda agreed. When they reached the stables, she rubbed down Bronwen, and put her in her box, then went with Randall to admire his new horse, a fine dark brown. 'He's only a youngster,' he told her. 'I'm schooling him for show jumping. I might sell him later, I shall just see. But I'll keep Bronwen, and breed from her.'

Amanda glanced from the handsome horse to the handsome boy. 'Then you still mean to stay on at Danesford?'

'I certainly do.' Randall's face hardened. 'I don't intend to get out, and leave Justin a clear field. He works like a mole, underground, so that you don't realize his next objective until it's too late. You know he's got the tenancy of Ridley's Farm? That had been promised to me. Afterwards, Father suggested that I might manage Northbrook, the home farm. But now Justin is talking about altering the house at Northbrook, for himself and Vanessa. I know what that means, that Justin intends to have Northbrook, as well as Ridley's. I believe that's been his aim all along. He can't afford to rent both farms now, but he's preparing the way for doing it after he's married. I'm being squeezed out all round. It was arranged that Justin should manage the estate until next spring, so I intend to be here then, and see that he doesn't stick to *that* job for keeps. Besides, Father wants me here. Justin rides rough-shod over most of his wishes, and he's not strong enough to stand up to him. He likes to have me around, so that I can tell him what Justin is getting up to.'

At that moment, they both heard the clatter of hoofs, and Justin rode through the archway, on Sigurd, the big black horse. They made a good-looking pair, a fine rider, superbly mounted. But Amanda looked at Justin with preju-diced and unfriendly eyes. He swung down from the saddle, and gave her a cool greeting.

'I've been telling Amanda my plans for my three horses,' said Randall, a sparkle of malice in his eyes.

'I hope you'll keep it in mind that horses don't always live up to your expectations,' commented Justin. The words were quiet, but there was a definite sting in them. Randall flushed angrily, and glowered after him as he led his horse across the yard. Amanda was uncomfortably conscious of another family row simmering below the surface.

'I must be going,' she said.

'Wait a minute, and I'll see you home.'

'No, please don't bother. It's only a short walk,' she told him, and left rather rapidly, glad to get away from the Warren atmosphere. She did not wholly like Randall, but her sympathies were with him. He was the most human of the Warrens; and whatever the cause, she would have resented that tone from Justin. But she thought Randall was foolish to stay at Danesford. As long as Justin was in charge, there seemed little Randall could do, except quarrel with his brother. He should look for a job, any job that would make him independent, give him experience, and improve his claim to help with the estate. Surely he would be happier proving to Justin, and everyone else, that he could do a real job of work, and do it well?

However, that was not Amanda's business, and Vanessa was. She wondered if Randall's surmises were correct. He had been right in his earlier prediction, that Justin wanted Ridley's Farm for himself, but it was rather surprising that Vanessa had said nothing to anyone, if she and Justin had decided where they were going to live.

She arrived home, to find Vanessa discussing that very subject. 'I always disliked the house at Ridley's,' she said. 'It's very old, and some of the rooms are poky. Northbrook is a much better house, and better placed, between Ridley's and Danesford. Mr Warren has agreed to our having it, so it's practically settled. It needs a lot doing to it, and we're going over it again tomorrow afternoon, so that I can decide on the alterations I want. Will you come too, Amanda? I'd like you to.'

'I was going for a walk, but I can do that any time. Justin won't mind my coming?'

'Of course not. Anyway, he won't want to go all over the house again.' Fine, thought Amanda, and decided to go equipped for a walk, so that she could leave the other two, after seeing the house, if she preferred it.

Justin arrived soon after lunch, and drove them down a twisting lane to Northbrook Farm. 'I've got a call to make. I'll leave you, and come back in an hour or so,' he said, giving Vanessa the key.

The house was a typical Northumbrian farmhouse of the better kind, built of grey stone, plain, solid, and substantial. It smelt close and rather musty inside, so their first action was to open downstairs windows wide, then Amanda looked round. The rooms were badly in need of repapering, but they were big and airy. 'With new paint and paper, gay curtains, and light carpets, they'd look fine,' she said.

Pleased by this praise, Vanessa took her upstairs to see the four bedrooms, bathroom, and box-room. Then they returned to the sitting-room, and looked about for somewhere to sit. There was nowhere except the window-seats, and they were thick with dust. 'My mac's used to rough treatment. We'll sit on that,' said Amanda.

She spread it on the window-seat, and they sat by the open window, talking. 'The bathroom will have to be completely done over. It's an ugly old relic,' said Vanessa. 'And I shall make the box-room into a second bathroom. The sitting-rooms are all right, but I want all that wandering back-place of kitchen, dairy and wash-house altered. I'd like one big kitchen, light and modern, and some of the remaining space could be made into a study for Justin, and a sun-lounge. We'll have to get an architect to make proper plans, and see what would be best. And I'll certainly have a wide paved terrace along the back, it's such a lovely view. And of course, central heating.'

Amanda listened, and wondered. Eventually she could not resist saying:

'But Vanessa, all that will cost an enormous amount, and I thought the Warrens were hard-up.'

'What you really mean is, who's going to pay, me or Justin, don't you?'

Amanda had carefully refrained from asking this question, but Vanessa knew her well enough to jump to the thought behind her words. 'All right,' she said, 'as a matter of simple curiosity, who will pay?'

'Justin will pay for having the house redecorated, and any repairs. If I want a lot of fancy extras, it's reasonable that I should pay for those, isn't it? After all, Justin will have to pay for all the farm improvements.'

'That's fair enough, as long as you're quite sure that Justin *will* pay for all his farm improvements.'

'Well, really!' Vanessa began indignantly, only to break off abruptly at the sound of a footstep on the gravel path. The two girls glanced at the open window behind them, then at one another, and Vanessa looked as guiltily caught out as Amanda felt.

A few seconds later, Justin appeared in the open doorway. As he looked at their self-conscious faces, his own was so guarded and inscrutable it was impossible to guess how much or how little he had overheard. Vanessa rushed into nervous speech: 'Amanda likes the house, but she thinks I want too many alterations.'

'They'd take time,' Amanda seconded her. 'It would be a good while before it was ready for you. We came by such twisting lanes, I'm not quite sure where we are.'

'If you come round to the back, you'll soon get your bearings,' suggested Justin. They went out of the front door, and round the house to a path at the back, where Vanessa wanted her terrace. It was a very fine view, fields sloping gently downhill, and a gleam of silver showing the course of the river. 'There's Danesford, below us on the right,' said Justin. 'You can just see it among the trees.'

'Oh, I know exactly where I am

now.' Amanda looked at the fields with the eyes of a farmer's grand-daughter. 'Those oats look good, and what fine Friesians! Didn't you say you were managing this farm?'

'Yes. My father had a manager here, but I didn't think he was much good, so I got rid of him.' Glancing sideways at Justin's hard-boned profile, Amanda thought that he could be more than a bit ruthless. 'It wasn't entirely his fault that the place was in bad shape,' he went on. 'It had been starved of money for so long that it could make only losses, not profit. I've spent a lot on it to get these results. Most of the money had to be borrowed, by my father, of course, as it's *his* farm; but I'm sure it will pay him in the end.' Justin's voice was cool and quiet, but it had a biting quality, which told Amanda that he must have heard her remark to Vanessa. Her cheeks flamed, and she could think of no adequate comment. It was the more difficult as he made no direct reference to her words, just left her to draw her own conclusions. 'Ridley's Farm adjoins this, higher up the hill,' he went on. 'I'd like to farm them both as one unit, and I may be able to do so later. Then, of course, I would have to pay for all these improvements, just as any other tenant would. However, I don't suppose that interests you, and we're keeping Vanessa waiting.'

He turned to go back, and Amanda followed him, for once without a single word to say. When he went into the house, she went straight back to the car. Justin had been altogether more master of the situation than she, putting her in the wrong very neatly, and rather unjustly. She and Vanessa had believed themselves to be alone, and if you couldn't talk freely to a sister, to whom could you talk? The fact that Justin could make her feel childish and absurd did not make her like him any more. When Vanessa's poodle came running down the path, ahead of the other two, she picked him up, and got into the back of the car, intending to ask Justin to drop her higher up the hill, so that she could go for a walk.

But as he got into the car, Justin said: 'I have to go to Ridley's next, and then I'm going to the plantation. Why don't you two go straight there? I may be some time, and it would be pleasanter than waiting in the car.'

Vanessa agreed, and Amanda did not mind where she went, provided she had no more of Justin's company. He stopped about half a mile higher up. They went through a gate, and along a cart-track, which ran along the side of the hill. The poodle danced along, delighted to be free, and so was Amanda. Tall trees shaded the path, the air was warm and pine-scented, and they had a wide view of fields and hills, already beginning to wear the brown and gold hues of autumn. Above them, the woodland stretched uphill and out of sight, a fine mixture of hard-woods and conifers.

'Let's sit down until Justin comes,' suggested Vanessa. They spread Amanda's mac on a patch of grass. Vanessa waved a fan of bracken, to keep away midges, which liked her pale skin better than Amanda's tan. The poodle snuffled around, and Amanda lay back on one elbow, enjoying the peace, but keeping a wary eye on the track, hoping that Justin would be a long time at the farm.

Time passed. Then she heard the snap of a twig above her, and turned to see him coming down through the wood. Watching him idly for a moment, the thought flashed through her mind that Justin was not only good-looking, but in some way seemed to fit into this hard, austere, yet beautiful countryside she loved so much.

It was only a fleeting thought, and in another moment she was on her feet, ready to move on. But Justin seemed in no hurry. He stood, looking up into the wood. 'There's some good timber up there, don't you think, Amanda?' he remarked. His tone was quite friendly, and she wondered if this was meant as an olive branch.

'I've been admiring it,' she answered,

equally amiably. 'It looks so much finer than an unbroken mass of conifers.'

'Much of it was my grandfather's work. He was a great believer in planting trees for future generations. Many of these trees won't be ready for cutting for a long time yet, but those at the far end should be ready in from six to ten years. It's a long time to wait, but do you, with your farming blood, feel it's justifiable to fell good trees before they've reached maturity?'

Amanda had already realized that this was no olive branch, but another of Justin's oblique attacks. Reluctantly, but honestly, she answered: 'It would be a shame.' Then, with a sudden spurt of rebellion at being put in the wrong again, she added: 'But I think people should come before trees.'

Justin turned abruptly away, and Amanda felt that she had scored one small point, at last. Vanessa displayed a midge bite on her wrist, and received indulgent sympathy from Justin. He was much nicer to Vanessa than to herself, thought Amanda, but he treated her rather as though she was a charming child, to be petted and taken care of. Vanessa might think that was love. Amanda did not. As they walked back along the track, she said: 'I was going for a walk, so you won't mind if I leave you now?'

'I thought you might both come back to Danesford for tea,' answered Justin. 'But just as you like.'

Amanda left them at the gate. She had had enough of Justin's company for one afternoon, and thought that, having scored his point, he was probably equally glad to be rid of her. She climbed to the top of the lane, and paused to get her breath, still very ruffled. She wondered if Justin had taken them to the plantation, just to force that admission from her, about felling trees. The only merit she would allow him was that he was clever, altogether too clever at putting other people in the wrong. Then she gradually became aware of the tawny fields and hedgerows below her, the open moor behind, the wind laden with peaty moor scents whipping her hair about her ears, and she dismissed thoughts of Justin, and took a twisting path through the heather.

It was nearly dark when she returned home. 'You should have come to Danesford with us,' said Vanessa. 'Mr Warren had tea with us, and was sorry not to see you. Randall has talked a lot about you, so I've promised to take you another day.'

5

When Amanda went to Danesford a couple of days later, she liked Mr Warren better than his wife, and the conversation was more interesting, mainly about an outbreak of sheep-stealing in the district. Amanda had heard about it from her grandfather, and could contribute her share of news, about which farms had suffered. Neither Ridley's nor Northbrook were among them, yet.

Seeing the whole family together, it was plain to Amanda that Mr Warren relied on his elder son, but loved the younger one far more. That was unlikely to make the relationship between the two any easier, with Randall trying to oust Justin from the management of their father's estate, and Justin equally anxious to keep a careful eye on his inheritance, to make sure that it was a good one, when the time came. She wondered how much Vanessa realized of these family cross-currents.

Soon after this visit, Vanessa told her family that she and Justin had made up their minds to live at Northbrook when they were married, but had not yet settled on a date for their wedding. Caroline was to be married some time in November, and they didn't want the two weddings to be more or less on top of one another, and did not know how long the alterations to Northbrook were likely to take. So it would probably be January or February, the following year.

Amanda listened with very mixed feelings. She was glad that several months would elapse before Vanessa was likely to be married, but work was to start on the house almost immediately, and that in itself seemed to make the marriage more of a settled thing. Everyone, except Amanda, regarded it as entirely settled, and even she was beginning to feel that it was almost inevitable. Vanessa was already discussing her wedding dress, and that of Amanda, as chief bridesmaid.

Since her parents' return, Amanda had had her father's company on some of her walks. He was as keen a walker as herself, and had the additional interest of gathering material for his book on Northumberland. Amanda doubted if the book would ever be published, but she had promised to provide some sketches for it. She enjoyed drawing, and was well aware of her own limitations. A good landscape was beyond her, but she could make exact and charming sketches of flowers, plants, buildings, and small details of buildings.

She was out on the moors alone one afternoon. Her parents had gone for a shopping trip, and she wanted to finish some flower sketches for the book. She was too absorbed in drawing to note the swiftly gathering clouds, until, glancing up, she saw an ominous mass of leaden clouds scurrying across the sky. She stuffed the sketching pad into her jacket pocket, and picked up the mac on which she had been sitting. Then the sky seemed to open, and a blinding sheet of rain descended. Amanda was well accustomed to Northumbrian weather, but this was more like a cloud-burst than an ordinary rain squall. The rising wind caught at her mac, almost whipping it out of her hands, and she was a good deal more than just damp, by the time she had managed to struggle into it. Her hand went to the pocket, feeling for her waterproof hood, and found only emptiness. She realized that she must have left it in the pocket of a jacket she had worn the previous day.

Cursing her own carelessness, she buttoned up her mac, looking around for any possible shelter. No light-weight mac was proof against such a deluge. But she knew exactly where she was, and knew that an empty shepherd's cottage was the only building within a mile. Even that was some distance away. She made for the only shelter in sight, the lea side of the nearest stone wall, and crouched down against it. She had been there for about five minutes, and her hair, feet and legs were already about as wet as they could be, when a rider suddenly loomed up through the blinding rain. The noise of it had drowned all sound of his approach. A moment later, Amanda realized it was Justin. She looked at him with disbelief and disgust, and hoped he was in too much of a hurry to see her.

But then he reined in his horse, jumped down, and walked towards her. Amanda stood up. Sopping wet and cold, she had precious little dignity left, but still felt that she would rather meet him erect than crouching down against the wall. As he looked at her expressive face, Justin's mouth twisted in an involuntary grin. 'Me, again!' he said. 'It's terrible, isn't it?' In spite of everything, answering laughter leapt into Amanda's eyes. Then he added: 'At least I can offer you shelter near by.'

'There's no shelter near here.'

'You don't know everything. Get on the horse, and let's get going.'

'I can't ride your horse, while you walk.'

'You can, and you will. My legs are longer, and can cover ground faster. Stop dawdling. I'm getting soaked as well as you.'

His arm behind her shoulders urged her onward, and in a few moments she was up on the horse, not entirely of her own volition. 'But this is the horse you said no one else could ride,' she exclaimed.

'You'll be all right while I'm here. You needn't be afraid.'

Amanda bit back an indignant denial, as Justin led the horse forward, his long stride covering the ground with surprising speed. Very soon, a cottage loomed up through the torrential downpour. Amanda recognized it as the shepherd's cottage, which had been empty for years. Even if they could get inside, it would prove but cold and miserable shelter. Justin and the horse stopped. Amanda slid down, and Justin gave her a key. 'Go inside, while I get Sigurd under cover. Leave the door on the latch.'

Greatly wondering, Amanda unlocked the door, pushed it open, and stepped into a small hall. There were doors on either side, one of them half-open. She pushed it fully open, and then stood gazing in sheer astonishment. In spite of the gloom from black skies outside, there was light enough to see a comfortably furnished room, rugs on the floor, a lamp on the table.

Swift steps came round the house, the front door slammed, and Justin's hand on her shoulder propelled her firmly into the room. He reached for a box of matches on the mantelpiece, and stooped to light an oil heater. 'Can't you even get out of your wet things?' he asked, glancing impatiently over his shoulder.

Feeling rather foolish, Amanda stopped staring, and unbuttoned her mac. 'I was startled. I thought this place had been empty for years,' she explained defensively. 'Who does live here?'

'No one. I furnished it as a handy stopping-place, and a useful shelter.' Justin pulled off his streaming leather jacket, and proceeded to crumple a newspaper into the grate, then added sticks, and set a light to them. When they blazed up, he added some small logs, straightened up, and looked at Amanda again. 'You *are* wet.'

'I've been as wet many a time before. Wetter,' she added with a sudden grin, remembering the day she fell into the river. With a soaking wet handkerchief, she tried to mop the rain-water from her soaked hair, which was running down her cheeks, then shivered uncontrollably.

Justin went out of the room, and returned with a towel. 'Rub your hair with this. It's probably dampish; things do get damp in an empty house, but it's better than nothing. And then you'd better get those wet shoes and stockings off.'

Amanda realized with surprise that he was genuinely concerned about her. Obediently, she rubbed her hair, while he added more logs to the fire. 'You must be pretty wet yourself,' she observed.

'A trifle damp, that's all. My riding clothes are proofed. Do get those wet shoes off.'

Amanda's shoes came off with a squelching sound. Her stockings soon followed. Justin rummaged in a drawer, and turned, holding out a large pull-over. 'This is the only spare garment I keep here, but at least it's dry, while all yours are soaked.' Amanda regarded it dubiously, and amusement gleamed again in Justin's eyes. 'I'm afraid it's not exactly becoming, but quite big enough for decency. I'll give you five minutes to get out of your own things, and into this,' he finished firmly, and departed.

Amanda hesitated, eyeing the pull-over, and then started to shiver again. The fire was burning well, the room was beginning to warm up, but she was chilled to the bone in her wet clothes. She pulled them off, and donned the pullover. It came down farther than some mini-dresses, and with the sleeves rolled up, it was a lot more comfortable than her wet things. There was no mirror in the room, but she could easily imagine the sketch she must look, tousled wet hair and all.

Justin returned, with a kettle, and set it on the fire. Amanda looked at him, a trifle warily. Now that she was dry, and beginning to feel warm again, she remembered their last meeting, that afternoon at Northbrook farmhouse. Between her indiscreet remark to Vanessa, and Justin's determination to make her regret it, they had been about equally angry with one another. But for the moment, at least, they seemed no longer enemies. The storm beat against the walls, making the little cottage seem a place of comfort and warmth, and Amanda was grateful enough to welcome a truce. 'I was sketching, and didn't notice the

131

storm blowing up,' she volunteered. 'I knew this cottage was not far away, but it's been deserted for so long.' She paused, dying to ask questions, but not sure if they were on good enough terms for that.

'I find it convenient sometimes,' he answered with his usual reserve. Then, glancing at her warm friendly expression, he enlarged: 'I have to cover a good deal of ground, and like to ride, when possible. This place has been a useful shelter before today.'

Looking round with interested eyes, Amanda thought it looked more than a mere shelter from the weather. The room had a snug, lived-in look, and a scatter of books and newspapers. With a swift flash of understanding, she thought, if she had to live in someone else's house, in an atmosphere of perpetual family discord, a place like this would be just what she most needed. Had Justin furnished it as a private refuge? Such a homely, rather shabby little place did not seem quite Justin's style, but how well did she really know him? Hardly at all; he seemed to surround himself with such an impenetrable shell of reserve. Innumerable questions crowded into her mind, but she had no wish to be snubbed for her curiosity, or to rouse their usual antagonism.

When the kettle boiled, Justin produced a tea-caddy and pot, cups and saucers, from a wall-cupboard. This shelter seemed very well-provisioned, a fact which seemed to confirm Amanda's speculations. 'It'll have to be dried milk, or none,' he told her. 'Which do you prefer?'

'None. I never do have milk.'

Justin poured out the tea, and produced a tin of biscuits from the cupboard. Having provided her with shelter, warmth and food, he did not exert himself to provide conversation as well, but sat looking as self-contained and reserved as ever. Trying a roundabout way towards satisfying her curiosity, Amanda asked: 'Is this cottage part of the Danesford estate?'

'Yes, almost on the edge of it.'

'It must be a good deal more extensive than I'd realized.'

'If it was less extensive, it would probably be more profitable.'

Profit, was that always his first thought? wondered Amanda. None the less, she knew that farmers on this sort of land could seldom afford high rents. 'How many farms have you?' she asked.

'Seven. Northbrook and Ridley's, and five others that are rented. I was on my way to see the tenant of the smallest farm, when this storm broke. I don't think I'll bother now.'

'It doesn't look as though it will go off for some time.'

'No; but my main reason is that this rain will have added urgency to his demands for drainage works.'

'Oh!'

Justin put down his cup. 'Last week, you told me that people were more important than trees.' Amanda gave him a glance of silent protest, which said very plainly, if she was willing to bury their differences for a while, why was he not equally willing? Ignoring it, he went on: 'I don't disagree, but unfortunately the choice is rarely so simple. If you had to choose between the demands of a spoilt boy, who thinks the world owes him an easy life, and those of a hill-farmer who is having a hard struggle to earn a living, which would you choose?'

Amanda knew there was only one honest answer, but she disliked Justin's way of describing his young brother. 'I don't know enough to judge,' she said.

'But you do judge,' Justin retorted, bitingly. He walked across to a bureau, unlocked it, and came back with a map in his hand. Unfolding it, he spread it out across Amanda's knees. Her eyes ran over it, and she realized that it must be a large-scale map of the Danesford estate. Standing beside her chair, and bending over the map, Justin went on: 'There's Danesford, down by the river, and here is this cottage. It was part of the farm I meant to visit today

135

— Staneshiel. And that name should tell another Northumbrian the sort of farm it is,' he observed, with a grim smile. 'A big farm in acres, but mainly poor land. The farmer is a man of my own age, John Roberts.'

'John Roberts, but I know him!' exclaimed Amanda. 'He's a friend of my cousin Frank, and I've met him occasionally over at Hesket, but not recently.'

'He probably hasn't much time for visiting. I've known him most of my life. He grew up at Staneshiel, the youngest of three boys. The older ones got out, but John stayed, and took over the tenancy, when his father died. He's very attached to the place, but I doubt if he'd have stayed, if he'd realized what he was letting himself in for. Staneshiel is a much poorer farm than in his father's day. Everything is in need of repair or replacement, buildings and drains. That's the fault of a landlord who refuses to face his responsibilities. As the landlord is my father, I don't enjoy saying this, but facts are facts.' Justin's voice was quiet and forceful, the brief clipped sentences following one another like hammer blows, and Amanda was suddenly aware of the passion underlying the flat words.

She looked quickly up into his face, leaning over her, and for the first time she realized that there was plenty of feeling locked in behind that quiet self-contained expression, that Justin was not nearly as cold-blooded as she had sometimes thought. 'John has struggled on for years, with an increasingly inefficient farm,' he continued. 'It brings him a bare living, not enough to pay for good, modern machinery. We were boys together, but these days, I'm ashamed to go up there, and face him. I'm glad of any excuse to put it off. If I could help him, even a little, it would be different. But my hands are tied.'

'I thought your father left the management of the estate entirely to you,' Amanda ventured, rather hesitantly.

'My powers are very limited, and

very temporary. Among other things, I can't prevent my father's paying off Randall's debts.'

Amanda was astonished at such frankness, from Justin of all people. She suddenly remembered the bitter little exchange she had heard between him and Randall, at the stables. 'Has Randall been backing horses?' she asked.

'Extensively and very unwisely. But that's a flea-bite compared with the debts that had to be settled when he finished college earlier in the summer — not much short of two thousand pounds.'

Amanda stared at him, almost unbelievingly. 'But how on earth could he spend that much?'

Justin shrugged. 'A car, a few wild parties and extravagant bets. Randall has a remarkable capacity for getting rid of money. But when I think of the difference that money could have made at Staneshiel — '

Prejudiced Amanda might be, but she hadn't a grudging or ungenerous impulse in her nature. 'If I'd known all this, I'd never have suggested you were mean with Randall,' she exclaimed. 'I'm sorry for the things I said that day at Ridley's.'

The hard lines of Justin's face broke into a smile that seemed to alter his entire personality. 'You'd only heard one side of it. It's perfectly true that my father did promise Ridley's to Randall, and I prevented his keeping that promise. I can use my own capital to stock it, while Randall would have needed money from the estate. It simply is not available, without borrowing at high interest rates, and Randall has not enough experience to justify that. And neither can we afford to sell timber at a loss, timber that will be worth considerably more in a few years time. John Roberts would understand, and may be willing to go on waiting. But he's only one of many. Unfortunately, my father is not really interested in land. If his tenants and his family all want money, then he'll always put his family first. Even now, when he realizes everything's in a mess, the money drains away from the land, Randall's debts, a grand wedding for Caroline, and I can't oppose things like that, when his health's so precarious.' Returning to the map, Justin's finger moved from one farm to another. This one needed new buildings, that one repairs to the farmhouse, and a better water supply. 'Obviously, the more a farm is starved of necessary capital, the less profitable it becomes. You know enough to understand that. Each time I go to Staneshiel, I expect John to tell me he's quitting. It might be difficult to find another good tenant, and you know what would happen to a farm like that, if it stayed empty for long, with bracken and gorse always in wait to swarm back over the fields.'

As she listened, Amanda became sharply aware of the insecurity behind the appearance of luxury and prosperity. With a quick impulse of sympathy, she wondered what kind of run-down, debt-burdened estate Justin might inherit. But hard on the heels of this came thoughts of Vanessa.

Justin seemed to have an uncanny perception of her withdrawal, and perhaps even the reason for it. The shutters came down over his face again, and the easy companionship that was growing between them vanished. Folding the map, he walked over to the window, and stood looking out for a few moments. 'The downpour's eased off to a thick drizzle,' he said, still with his back turned. 'It'll probably last for the rest of the day. I think I'll ride back to Danesford, get out my car, and run you home.'

'Oh, please don't bother. My clothes will be nearly dry, and I don't mind ordinary rain. I'll walk home.'

'It's no bother at all. Vanessa's dining with us, so I can collect her, when I take you home.' Justin's voice was cool, polite, and indifferent again. 'All the paths will be a morass, and your shoes still wet,' he added, getting into his jacket as he spoke. Then, not waiting for more protests, he was gone.

Amanda pushed her feet into still wet shoes, and went over to the window. Justin was just leading his horse through the small gateway. She saw him swing himself up into the saddle, and then man and horse disappeared into the mist and drizzle. She turned, and looked round the room for anything she could do. Collecting the tea-things, she explored the back regions, and found a scullery, with a sink and one cold tap. She heated more water on the fire, and washed the dishes. Her thoughts were strangely mixed. For the very first time, she had enjoyed talking to Justin, and felt in full agreement with him. She liked open people who spoke their minds, and, for once, Justin had shown an astonishing unreserve. She was angry with herself for having destroyed the harmony of the last hour, but Justin's very outspokenness had inevitably brought thoughts of Vanessa.

She had often accused him of harping on the subject of money. Now, she admitted that it was not money itself that was so important to him, but only money in relation to Danesford. He really loved the place, and loved it with a feeling of responsibility, unlike the rest of his family. He was not half as hard and invulnerable as he seemed, and she had begun to like him, until she remembered Vanessa. She could sympathize with Justin's feelings about Danesford, but Vanessa was her step-sister. The more she knew about the Warren finances, the more she felt that Justin was making use of Vanessa, that he saw her as the perfect answer to his problems.

Perhaps he felt that was justifiable. Perhaps he thought he was giving as much as he was getting. Vanessa loved the beauty of Danesford, and had enough of her mother in her to be thrilled by the idea of marrying into one of the oldest families in the county. But that was only one bit of Vanessa, the least important bit. She was generous, warm-hearted, and impulsive, incurably romantic, and too easily swayed by any stronger personality.

Amanda still felt that Vanessa needed to be saved from her romantic self-delusions, and that Justin was not in love with her. He had talked very freely about Randall, and about the estate, but withdrawn into himself the moment she even thought about Vanessa. She could not help suspecting that he knew he had a good case, where his family and the estate were concerned; but no defence where Vanessa was concerned.

She put the dishes away, found that her skirt and pullover were nearly dry, so changed back into them, and all the time her thoughts ran on. Why had Justin bothered to defend himself to her? He'd never attempted it before, but seemed totally indifferent to her opinions. Pride, perhaps. But, remembering his reluctance to go to Staneshiel empty-handed, Amanda thought he was more sensitive, more easily hurt than he would allow people to guess. She looked thoughtfully around the room, small, homely, and unpretentious. It did not fit her ideas about Justin. Was that because her ideas were all wrong? This room seemed the absolute opposite to the luxurious elegance of Danesford. Could that have been Justin's object, a place of his own, an antidote to family discord and extravagance? There were other provisions in the cupboard; books and writing materials on the bureau. Definitely more than a mere, occasional shelter.

Feeling for a handkerchief, Amanda found her forgotten sketching-pad. Her sketches were crumpled and damp, but not altogether hopeless. She held them to dry in front of the fire, then spread each one out on Justin's map. She was still drying them when Justin came back. He glanced at the array on the map, and his face sprang into sudden life and interest. 'So that's what you were doing, when the storm broke! They're good, an excellent collection of local flowers. Finish drying them. There's no hurry.'

He leaned back against the table, watching as she held the last two sketches up to the fire, and whistling softly to himself. After a few seconds, Amanda's ear caught the air, and she turned in quick surprise. 'Fair Flower of Northumberland! You know that old ballad?'

'Why should that surprise you? I'm as much Northumbrian as you.'

'Yes, of course. My grandfather taught it to me, long ago, but it's not very appropriate to these,' and she gestured at the sketches. 'After all, that fair flower was an unfortunate girl, whose lover only wanted to make use of her.'

The words were lightly and carelessly spoken, with no thought of their aptness, until she saw Justin's face lose its friendly animation. He looked at her bleakly, saying nothing; and for once Amanda was completely at a loss for words. She got to her feet, collected her sketches, and got into her mac. Justin occupied himself in raking out the fire, and she looked at his back, longing to say something to wipe out the effect of her careless words, but could think of nothing. Still silently, she followed him out of the cottage.

The cart-track leading from it was rutted and very muddy, and Justin had to concentrate on driving. Once on the road, it was only a short drive to Greystones, and Vanessa was ready and waiting for him there. Amanda thanked him again, and when they had gone, went upstairs for a bath, and a change of clothes.

She took time, trying to sort out her thoughts, which were tugged in two opposite directions. Because she had liked Justin today, she was readier to believe that Vanessa *might* be in love with him. For the same reason, she would have liked to believe that he was in love with Vanessa, but she could not. The fact that he would defend himself about Randall, but not about Vanessa, although he certainly knew what she thought, all inclined Amanda to this conclusion. If Justin loved Danesford enough to marry money in order to save it from ruin, she could respect such a motive, as she would not mere greed for money. But Vanessa deserved better than that. Amanda was more realistic than Vanessa, but she believed in love, and she was afraid that Vanessa would be getting less than the best.

All the same, she resolved to stop trying to meddle in the affair. She had done no good. She had lost much of her old power to influence Vanessa, and had been mistaken about Justin's character. All she had done was to annoy them both, and make herself look, and feel, rather silly.

6

The day after the storm was grey and damp, but no longer raining. Amanda spent a good part of the morning at her books, and went for a walk in the afternoon. She took the footpath which crossed Ridley's Farm. For various reasons, she had avoided that path, ever since the day she encountered Justin there; but today she chose it deliberately, as an act of belated justice. She knew there was no danger of meeting Justin again, as he was elsewhere with Vanessa. There were things she wanted to see for herself.

After yesterday's deluge, the hills were full of the haunting sound of running water, and the grass was so loaded with moisture that Amanda's feet were soon soaked again. Giving her curiosity full rein, she left the path, and wandered across several fields. Everywhere, she recognized evidence of neglect, of a careless farmer, or a bad landlord. Probably both, as a neglectful landlord might find it difficult to get a good tenant.

She returned to the footpath, and stood for some time gazing across the fields. Justin was certainly not taking on an easy job here. How much money would be needed to improve this poor grazing, to repair buildings and drains, and generally make it into a thriving farm again? And then there would be the cost of stock and machines. Where would the money come from? The answer still seemed unpleasantly obvious, but Amanda was now pulled in two directions. She came of farming stock, and had acquired from her grandfather strong feelings about land. She appreciated the importance of keeping it in good heart, and understood a farmer's love of his own land. With a feeling of sheer exasperation, with herself and things in general, she decided to go back to the house and her books. Plants were simpler, and much less confusing than people.

Next morning, she went into the local town with her father. He wanted to go to the library, and she to do some oddments of shopping. She had finished some time before she had arranged to meet him again, and decided to fill in time by getting coffee. It was a Saturday morning, so the café was rather full. Looking round for a vacant place, Amanda noticed a face that seemed vaguely familiar. She looked a second time, and recognized John Roberts, of Staneshiel. Impulsively, she went over to his table. At sight of her friendly smile, he got to his feet, wearing a slightly puzzled expression. Amanda's smile widened. 'You've forgotten me, and I don't wonder. I'm Amanda Carr, and I've met you with my cousin, Frank Deane.'

'Of course! I knew I knew you, but couldn't place you,' he answered, looking relieved. 'This is my fiancée, Janet Martin. Do join us.'

The two girls smiled at one another, and Amanda sat down. 'If I'd known you had company, I wouldn't have butted in. But I didn't know you were engaged.'

'It's quite new, only since last week-end,' Janet told her.

Amanda ordered coffee, her mind rapidly considering this news, wondering if Justin knew of it. 'Staneshiel's a lonely farm. You won't mind that?' she asked Janet.

'No. My grandfather's a farmer.'

'So is mine.'

'But Hesket's a good farm,' said John Roberts.

'Yes,' Amanda agreed, rather uncertainly. 'I don't know much about Staneshiel.'

'It could be a good farm, too,' Janet interposed swiftly, 'if the landlord wasn't an old skinflint. You should see the house! Primitive's the only word for it.'

'But you are prepared to live there?'

'As long as John wants to keep the farm, I'll put up with the house.'

'Good for you!' Amanda applauded.

'But you shouldn't have to put up with it.'

'Well, we're hoping that things may improve. Mr Warren, John's landlord, is no longer fit to manage things himself, and his son's marrying money, so there might be a bit in it for us.'

'Justin's marrying my sister,' said Amanda, very hastily. There was a startled silence. John Roberts turned brick-red, but Janet seemed to be trying not to laugh. Amanda hastened to add: 'It's all right. You didn't say anything tactless, but I thought I'd better warn you. Actually, Vanessa's my step-sister. That's why we have different surnames. She inherited money from her uncle. I haven't a penny, myself. Vanessa's the most generous person, only the farm doesn't belong to Justin. It's his father's.'

'I don't wish Mr Warren any ill,' said Janet. 'But he isn't a good landlord.'

'No, he isn't, and that's a fact.' John joined in heavily. 'I wouldn't stay at Staneshiel, except that I've been there all my life, and it would be a wrench to leave.'

'And you think that Justin would be a better landlord, if — ?' suggested Amanda.

He gave her a startled look, but answered: 'That's the main reason why I stay. Justin's not like his father. He's like his grandfather, and old Mr Warren was one of the best.' John smiled a slow smile, which brought sudden charm to his personality. 'We're exactly the same age, Justin and I. One day, when we were kids, his grandfather had left him at Staneshiel, and we got into some mischief. My father, who had a quick temper, walloped us both. But then, when Mr Warren called for Justin, he apologized for doing it. Mr Warren looked at the pair of us, and asked if we'd earned a thrashing. We said yes, so he just laughed, and said: 'Send John to play with Justin, next time. And if he gets into mischief there, I promise I'll do the same.' He was always fair, and never thought he was better than his neighbour.'

Amanda looked at the pair with keen interest. John was dark, and a trifle stolid looking, but his eyes were wide-awake and intelligent. Janet was fair and friendly, and seemed to have a very cheerful disposition. She would probably need it, thought Amanda. 'What's wrong with the house?' she asked.

'Everything.' Janet gave her a considering look, then added: 'We're just going up there, now. Why not come with us, and see for yourself? Stay for lunch, if you don't mind it being a bit rough.'

'I'd love to,' exclaimed Amanda. 'But I'll have to tell my father I'm not returning with him. Can you wait ten minutes?'

She hurried to the library, found her father still there, then went on to the car park, where Janet and John were waiting, beside his elderly estate car. She liked them both, but suspected that Janet's invitation was partly based on the hope that she might be able to influence Vanessa, to help in some way.

Staneshiel farmhouse was small, but stoutly and solidly built of grey stone. John Roberts opened the door for the two girls, but then Janet took charge. Dumping her shopping-bag, she took Amanda on a tour of the house. 'The living-room,' she said, opening the door of a fair-sized room, with old-fashioned, well-worn furnishings. 'This is the dining-room, but John doesn't use it. Now, come and see the kitchen.'

Amanda followed her in, and John silently brought up the rear. Amanda stood in the middle of the stone-flagged kitchen, and looked around at the chipped sink, with its one tap; the small, badly placed windows; and the ancient, solid fuel cooker. 'No hot water, no electricity, and not even much daylight. Is there a bathroom?'

'What do you think?' retorted Janet, with scorn. 'The lavatory's outside the back door, but at least it's got water.'

John cleared his throat. 'If neither of you need me, I've plenty of work waiting for me outside. I'll run you home, Amanda, if you let me know when you're going.'

'Oh, no, I'll walk. I like walking, and would hate to waste your time.'

John departed, wearing an air of relief. Janet's face softened, as she looked after him. 'Poor John! He's ashamed of bringing me to a place like this. He hasn't insisted on my putting up with it. He says, if I can't stand the house, he'll give up the farm, and try for a job. But he loves Staneshiel, in spite of all its drawbacks. Besides, there's not much choice. He knows nothing but farming. He might get better money and a better house as a farm worker, but he's used to being his own master. And he's stuck it out for so long, he might as well hang on a bit longer.'

'You mean that, if Mr Warren had another heart attack and died, things might be better?' said Amanda bluntly.

'John wouldn't thank me for putting it that way, but I know he thinks it; and can you blame him? Oh, well, come and see it all.'

She took Amanda to see the larder, the dark, stone-flagged wash-house, and the bedrooms, with sloping ceilings, one blotched by damp patches, showing that the roof needed mending. Returning to the kitchen, Janet started to prepare lunch, with Amanda helping. 'If you'll do the spuds and this cauliflower, I can get on with the pie. I come most week-ends, and see that John has at least two good meals in the week. I know he won't bother to do much cooking himself.' Janet was a real dynamo of energy, and could work at top speed, while talking at the same time. 'John's written to Justin Warren, to tell him he's going to get married, and wants some improvements to the house, but he's not very hopeful. That roof will have to be mended before winter, and that's flat. We ought to have hot water and a bathroom, too. We've not got much money, and what we have would be better spent on farm stock or

158

machinery. That would be ours, while the house never will be, and we might not even stay here for long. I'll put up with things as they are for a while, but not for ever. If we had a couple of children, and no more money coming in, I'd feel very differently.'

Amanda peeled potatoes, listened, and agreed. She wondered whether it would do any good to bring Vanessa up here. Vanessa would compare it with her own lavish plans for Northbrook, and certainly be shocked by the comparison. Whether it would achieve any practical results was a different thing.

When John returned, and washed at the kitchen sink, she told him that Janet had invited her to their wedding, and that she would love to come. She added: 'I think you're a very lucky man.'

'I know I am. I only wish I had something better to offer Janet. But I'm hopeful that things will improve. If Justin stays in control, I'm sure they will.'

'He's done nothing for you, so far,'

retorted Janet. 'Like father, like son, I say.'

'Justin spoke to me about this farm, a couple of days ago,' Amanda said slowly. 'He was on his way here when that storm broke, and he said he was glad of an excuse to put it off, because he felt ashamed to face you.'

'He's no call to feel like that,' exclaimed John. 'I've never blamed *him*. And if he's sorry for me, I'm sorry for him.' Janet snorted derisively, but John went on with unexpected firmness. 'I know what he has to contend with. He's got far more than I'll ever have, but he was trained by his grandfather to feel that Danesford was a fine inheritance, and a trust as well. For years, he's had to stand by and watch it being bled white, by a step-mother who's always resented him. A few more years of that, and it won't be an inheritance, only a mill-stone round his neck.'

Janet continued to look sceptical, but Amanda asked: 'Does Mrs Warren resent Justin?'

'That's my impression. He never talked about her, but I knew, in the way kids do, that he'd been far happier living with his grandfather. I'm not suggesting that she ever ill-treated him, only that she resented the fact that he was the heir, and not her own son. And it's my belief she enjoys making the money fly all the more, because she thinks Justin will have to pay in the end.'

After lunch, Janet started on the dishes. Then there was a knock at the door. 'Would you see who it is?' asked Janet. 'I'm up to my elbows in suds. Tell them John's somewhere round the farm.'

Amanda obliged, opened the door, and found Justin there. She stared at him, caught off-balance by surprise. Then self-conscious colour flooded her cheeks, and she felt quite unreasonably guilty at being found there. Justin looked as startled as she felt. 'Amanda!' he exclaimed.

Steps came along the hall, and she turned to see Janet. 'It's Justin Warren,' she told her. 'Justin, this is John's fiancée, Janet Martin.'

'Good afternoon,' said Janet, looking Justin up and down, in a distinctly belligerent fashion. 'You'll be wanting John. I don't think he's far away. I'll go and find him, if you'll wait inside.'

She departed. Justin stepped into the hall, and looked at Amanda silently, with an odd expression in his eyes. Wondering if he resented her being there, and thought her interfering, she rushed into explanations. 'I met John in a café in Thurston this morning. We had coffee together, and then they asked me to come back with them. When you talked about this farm, you didn't say that John was getting married. Did you know?'

'Not until yesterday,' said Justin heavily. 'But I've often wondered what would happen, if John did decide to marry. Fifty years ago, a country girl might have thought this a reasonable house, but few would take it on now. What do you think of this girl?'

'One of the best,' answered Amanda.

A second later, Janet reappeared. 'John won't be long,' she told Justin. 'In the meantime, you're the very person I wanted to see. Will you come into the kitchen?'

Justin went, almost meekly. Having learnt something about Janet's forceful character and forthright speech, Amanda felt unexpectedly sorry for him. She stood in the kitchen doorway, and listened to Janet holding forth on the shortcomings of the house. She had a good case, and made the very most of it. Justin began to look both badgered and guilty. Amanda sensed that he hated to say no, where he knew that he ought to be saying yes, but would not make any promises which his father might refuse to keep. All he did say, when Janet paused for breath, was: 'I'll do what I can. The roof must be repaired, of course. But if nothing more can be done, what then?'

Janet hesitated, obviously wondering if she could put pressure on him, by saying she would refuse to live there. Then she answered honestly: 'If you mean, would I refuse to marry John, then the answer's no. He doesn't want to leave Staneshiel, so I'd just try to put up with it.'

Justin broke into his rare smile, which lent undeniable charm to his face. Before he could speak, John came in. The two men greeted one another, in a friendly fashion, and exchanged a little farming shop. Then there was a pause. They looked at one another, and John fidgeted uncomfortably. 'Miss Martin has been telling me everything that's wrong with this house,' said Justin slowly and carefully. 'I think she's quite right to refuse to live here, unless we'll agree to make several improvements.'

'I never said any such thing,' exclaimed Janet indignantly. 'Now, did I, Amanda?'

John put a large, restraining hand on her arm. 'Just be quiet for a bit, Janet, and let Justin and me settle this.' The two men looked at each other again. A slow smile spread up into John's blue eyes, and was reflected in Justin's grey ones.

'If I tell my father that Miss Martin won't live in the house as it is; that if you're forced to choose between Staneshiel and the girl, you'll choose the girl, then we must ask ourselves if we can hope to get another tenant as good as you. Personally, I think it would be far cheaper to spend money on the house, than to risk getting a bad tenant, or perhaps none. And, of course, we should get a grant towards the house improvements. I'm afraid the farm would be more difficult, but let's have a look round, and talk it over.' As they went out together, Justin looked back at Amanda. 'If you're in no hurry, I can give you a lift home, when I come back.'

When they had gone, the two girls looked at one another. 'Well,' said Janet, reflectively, 'I can see what John means. He's not so bad, really, and that's quite a good line to take. Do you think he'll get anything out of Mr Warren?'

'I don't know, but from now on, I think I'd leave it to John. They obviously understand each other very well.'

Janet returned to her washing-up. Amanda dried the dishes very thoughtfully. She had been strangely moved by the little scene she had witnessed. Seeing Justin's difficulties, in human terms, before her eyes, had brought them home to her much more forcibly. And she could not help noting and liking the terms of easy, equal friendship on which the two men met. John had said that old Mr Warren never thought himself better than his neighbours. Neither, apparently, did Justin; and she was ashamed of having thought him a snob.

It was over an hour before Justin returned. He was alone, and only looked in to say good-bye to Janet, and ask Amanda if she would like a lift. She accepted, and they drove in silence for a short distance. Then Justin stopped the car, but still did not speak. He sat gazing absently at the landscape spread out below them. Amanda's eyes followed his, and she realized that this was just where she had stopped for breath, the afternoon she had left Justin and

Vanessa, after their visit to Northbrook Farm. She had been furious with Justin, after their verbal battle, in which he had won most of the points. That was only just over a week ago. She could hardly believe it, her ideas had changed so completely. She glanced at Justin's preoccupied face, still obscurely anxious that he should not think her visit to the farm interfering. 'I met John quite by accident,' she said hesitantly. 'I hope you don't think I was prying.'

'The thought never occurred to me,' he exclaimed, and smiled at her without reservations. 'I agree with you about the girl. She seems to be exactly what John needs. You think she really would take on the house and farm, just as they stand?'

'Yes I do. But she — '

'Shouldn't have to. No, of course she shouldn't. Well, I'll do what I can. I think I can make my father see that it's in his own interest to keep a man like John. Unfortunately, he will often make the right decision, and then let himself be talked out of it.'

'By Randall?'

'And his mother. And this time they'll have a real grievance. There's only one way, just now, that we can find the money to pay for all the improvements needed at Staneshiel. We'll have to sell timber — those trees I refused to have felled, in order to start Randall in farming.' Justin indicated the woodland, stretching down the hill to their left, and below them. 'You can imagine what they'll make of that.'

'Oh!' said Amanda.

Justin glanced at her quickly. 'You think I'm unfair to Randall. He's got good brains, and he's had a good training, but he lacks experience, and he's been brought up to be arrogant. If he started to farm on his own now, he'd lose money, lots of it, and we simply cannot afford to finance expensive mistakes. What Randall most needs is a dash of humility, the ability to admit that he can be wrong.' He gave Amanda a quick glance, and it flashed across her mind that he was wondering if she was a little in love with Randall, and might resent his words. 'I suppose Randall's told you that all I'm interested in is making certain I inherit a prosperous estate?' he added, his eyes suddenly bleak and bitter. 'Even if it were true, I can't see that it would be so contemptible. Most of our money comes from the land. I'd rather see it spent on giving the tenants a fair deal, and keeping the land in good heart, than watch it squandered on gambling, half a dozen cars, and all round extravagance.

'I lived with my grandfather for several years, when I was a child. He always treated me as his successor, as well as his grandson, and spent a lot of time trying to make sure that I would carry on the place, as he would have liked to see it. He had a great sense of continuity and tradition. I remember his saying: 'My father planted those trees, but you'll probably be the one to harvest them. Don't forget to plant more, for your grandchildren.' He trained me to think of Danesford as a trust, carrying responsibility to the land; to those who work the land; and to those who will come after us. I was too young to understand then, but I've seen the results of a very different attitude, since then. All I can do now is try to make the place pay, any old way at all. I'm sometimes tempted to chuck it, and go a long way away. But I know Randall's just waiting for such an opportunity, and I can easily imagine the results of a few years of his management.'

'But surely your father can see that you're right?'

'Yes, but he's not really interested in land. And Randall has always been his favourite, of the three of us. The years I spent with my grandfather, when I was a child, left a gap between us that's never been completely bridged. I've often wondered if he thought my mother might not have been killed, if she hadn't tried to shield me, when the car crashed.'

'I didn't know you were in that car smash!'

'I got off lightly, with a few cuts and bruises.' Amanda's eyes went to the long, faint scar in his cheek, about which she had once questioned Vanessa. They sat in silence, both deep in thought. Amanda wondered why Justin was talking so frankly. She had been surprised by his candour, that other day, in the shepherd's cottage, but that had been self-justification. There was something different about his manner today, as though he was asking, not for bare justice, but for understanding, and perhaps liking.

'Will your father agree to sell the timber, when you wouldn't let him do it for Randall?' she asked.

'I'm not sure. That's why I prompted John to give him something of an ultimatum. John obviously deserves a better deal. If that isn't enough, then Father has to consider what sort of tenant he could hope to get, with the place in its present condition. And the cost of improvements to Staneshiel would be a flea-bite, compared with the money needed to start Randall at Ridley's, in the style he would expect.'

'I hope you get something for them,' said Amanda, with impulsive warmth. 'I know you'll do everything possible.'

Justin's head turned sharply. Their eyes met, and a glow of feeling suddenly shone between them. 'Exonerated?' he asked.

Amanda did not pretend to misunderstand. 'I was judging without knowing the facts. I was wrong, and I'm sorry for some of the things I said.'

Justin said nothing, but he put his hand over hers. The warm, friendly touch of his fingers took Amanda's breath away. With a cold shock of dismay, she realized that she was on the verge of falling in love with Justin. Then he glanced at his wrist-watch, gave a startled exclamation, and removed his hand from hers. 'I had no idea it was that time! I was to have called for Vanessa half an hour ago.' He leaned forward and started the car.

The mention of Vanessa completed Amanda's dismay. She realized that, all the time they had sat talking companionably, she had forgotten Vanessa's existence. She could not have spoken if she had tried. In ten minutes they had reached the cottage. She got out of the car, and said good-bye, without daring to look at Justin. Vanessa came out of the door, as she reached it. 'I didn't make Justin late,' Amanda told her. 'That was a tenant with problems.'

'Most of them have problems,' returned Vanessa, very light-heartedly.

Amanda watched them drive way, then went up to her room. She felt slightly stunned and dazed, as though someone had just hit her over the head. She was much too susceptible, she told herself. Vanessa had twitted her with having been in love half a dozen times. Actually, it was only four times, and each time she had only gone half-way in, then found herself heading back for the shore, a little disappointed that it had not been the real thing, but much more relieved to find herself still heart-whole. And she'd better head back again this time, she told herself. It would be sheer disaster to fall in love with Justin.

She had been astonished, earlier that day, at the speed with which they had slipped from hostility into friendship. Then, only minutes later, the mere touch of his fingers had gone to her head like wine. She must not, must not, go from friendship to love, with equal speed, she told herself, still badly shaken by the effect of his light, casual touch.

7

Amanda was not easily daunted, but the discovery that she was on the brink of falling in love with the man who was engaged to her step-sister, and whom she had heartily disliked such a short time before, was a little too much, even for her. During the evening, she had a telephone call from her grandfather, to say that her grandmother had fallen and hurt her knee, not badly, but enough to prevent her getting about. Amanda instantly made the offer she knew he was hoping for, to stay with them for a while, and lend a hand. She would have offered, in any case, but felt that this was exactly what she needed, a breathing space, time to argue herself back to commonsense.

Her father drove her to Hesket next morning, and she received the warmest of welcomes. Her grandmother's knee was swollen and sore, but there was nothing wrong with it that time and rest would not cure. Her grandparents were as glad to have her company as her help, and she had plenty of occupation. The bungalow was easily kept clean and tidy, and Mr Deane was handy and ready to help, but no cook. When there was time, he enjoyed walking round the farm with her, showing her various improvements, and pointing out anything he thought was less well done than when he was in charge.

Amanda had brought some books with her, intending to study in the evenings, but when she was alone, no one to claim her attention, her thoughts were all tugged in one direction. She told herself that she had become ridiculously engrossed with Justin, first because she disliked and distrusted him, and then because she realized that she had been unjust, and regretted it. She had built up a very different picture from her original one; a child who had lost his mother very young, but was happy with his grandfather, absorbing all his ideas. Then a small boy, taken from that pleasant life to live with a step-mother who resented his existence, and a half-brother and sister who were loved and spoiled as he never had been. And now a young man, fighting bitterly to save a loved inheritance from ruin, opposed at every turn by the rest of his family. Sympathy and understanding had made her suddenly realize that he was, in his own way, an extremely attractive young man. That was all it was, that and her ridiculous susceptibility, Amanda told herself, and very soon managed to reason herself into a calmer and happier frame of mind.

On Wednesday afternoon, she went for a walk on the moors. She had a sketching-pad in her pocket, and sat down to draw a deserted shepherd's cottage. There was nothing very special about it, but it had taken her fancy, being plain and sturdy, almost as much a part of the landscape as the stones on the hillside. She drew in a line of hills for background, and surveyed it with a feeling of satisfaction. Getting to her feet, she was surprised to see a golden Labrador turn a curve in the path, and come trotting towards her. A moment later, Justin followed him. Amanda stood staring, shocked into immobility by the wild tumult in her heart. 'Your grandfather told me I'd find you somewhere along here,' he greeted her, then added: 'This must be quite a unique occasion, surely?' and she saw unexpected laughter in his eyes.

All Amanda's usual self-possession seemed to have deserted her. She could only stammer: 'Unique?'

'To meet you in the hills, and actually bone dry!'

A spark of answering laughter leapt into Amanda's eyes. 'I do seem to make a habit of it. Is Vanessa with you?'

'No. I came with a warning, and you mustn't tell her you've seen me. She's planning a surprise party for your birthday tomorrow, bringing your presents, and a fancy birthday tea. It will only be the two of us, as your father said your grandmother might not want a crowd, but I thought it might be a good idea to warn you. You might have gone out, like today, or be in the middle of something, and not welcome interruptions. Vanessa's gone to a lot of trouble, and I'd hate her to be disappointed.'

His voice softened unconsciously on the last words, and pain slashed savagely at Amanda's heart. She thrust her hands hard down in her pockets, struggling for command of herself. Her eyes fell on the dog, standing quietly beside Justin. 'Is he yours? I've never seen him before.'

'He's rather young and frisky, and Vanessa's poodle is scared of him, so he mostly gets left at home.'

Amanda held out her hand to the dog, and began to make friends with him, glad of this occupation for eyes and hands. After a few minutes, Justin asked: 'What were you drawing, when I came along? Had you finished it?' Silently,

Amanda gave him the sketching-pad, and he looked from the drawing to the cottage. 'M'm, a typical Northumbrian farm cottage, and you've got the absolute feel of it. I like it. Is it meant for your father's book? I suppose you couldn't spare it?'

'Of course. Take it. I can easily do another.'

Justin carefully tore off the sketch, and put it in his pocket-book, Amanda watching with feelings that were half-pleasure and half-pain. Then they turned to walk back again. Justin seemed quite content to walk in silence, but Amanda was too self-conscious. Searching her mind for a safe topic, she remembered the circumstances of their last meeting, and asked: 'Have you got anything settled about Staneshiel?'

She regretted the question, as Justin's face lost its relaxed expression. 'No, nothing yet. I'd feel more confident, if Randall didn't insist on taking a hand. My father's much better, but not well enough for continuous arguments and badgering. If Randall should win, then John may have the unpleasant choice of eating his words, or giving up his farm. He'll probably wish he'd never listened to me.'

Amanda longed to express her sympathy, but was afraid to, lest her face showed her feelings too clearly. When they reached the bungalow, Justin refused to come in, saying he could not spare the time, so she said good-bye, and went in alone. She had to tell her grandfather the reason for Justin's call, and he readily agreed to look completely taken by surprise, when Vanessa arrived, and not to tell his wife anything about it.

Amanda went to her bedroom, and sank down on the bed, her face buried in her hands. All her carefully built up defences had been demolished by that first unexpected sight of Justin. She knew that she was not merely on the brink of falling in love, but loved him in a way that was terrifyingly different from anything she had ever felt before. She still believed that Justin was not really in love with Vanessa, but her love for him now accepted him as he was. She felt that he was genuinely fond of Vanessa, but probably loved Danesford more than he would ever love any human being. To Amanda, that was wrong, but when it had been bred into him from his earliest years, when most of his human relationships had been unsatisfactory, it was not really surprising.

Now that she was in love with Justin herself, Amanda found it easier to believe Vanessa was in love with him. Vanessa was always drawn to determined people, who knew their own minds; and Justin was certainly that. It might even be a happy marriage. Vanessa was not critical enough to distinguish between warm affection, and real love; and if Danesford was Justin's real love, she was not likely to have any human rival in his affections.

And what of herself? Amanda asked, and could find no comforting answers. She had been a little in love before, and got over it very quickly, but those feelings had been pale in comparison with this overwhelming love. With Justin engaged to Vanessa, she was bound to see them often together. She had never been much good at playing a part, so how was she to conceal her feelings from Vanessa, and from Justin himself? Tomorrow's party loomed up before her as a major ordeal, which must be got through somehow.

After lunch next day, she put on a light summer dress, which looked fresh and pretty, but with no suggestion of having prepared for a celebration. She inspected herself in the mirror, and was surprised and relieved to see that unhappiness had made no noticeable difference to her looks. Fortunately, she had not long to wait. Vanessa arrived early, carrying a handsome birthday cake, and Justin followed, bearing flowers and an armful of presents, from her parents, as well as Vanessa. Opening these gave Amanda a welcome occupation, while Vanessa chattered gaily about anything and nothing.

Justin was rather silent, and Amanda, not trusting herself overmuch, kept her eyes from straying often in his direction, but she was acutely and achingly aware of him all the time.

After tea, Mr Deane suggested taking Justin round the farm. Vanessa decided that she and Amanda would go too. Mr Deane took firm possession of Justin, and the two girls dropped behind. 'You won't have heard that Mr Warren's been very poorly,' said Vanessa. 'Mrs Warren had to call the doctor in yesterday afternoon, and he said he must take things more quietly. Not that he does much,' she added.

Amanda wondered if family arguments were to blame. She was even unkind enough to wonder if it might be a diplomatic relapse, to allow Mr Warren to postpone a difficult decision, and to use his health as an excuse for doing nothing about Staneshiel. She came out of these thoughts to find that Vanessa was talking about Caroline's wedding. 'She's not sure if her father will be well enough to give her away. Justin says he'll probably be landed with the job. He doesn't seem to want it. I don't know why.'

'He probably thinks she shouldn't insist on an elaborate wedding, at the present time.'

'Any girl has a right to a lovely wedding.' Vanessa sounded mildly outraged. 'After all, she only gets married once.'

'Knowing Caroline, I rather doubt that,' said Amanda dryly.

Vanessa giggled. 'Maybe you're right. But you are determined to dislike the Warrens, aren't you?'

'I don't like Caroline. I think Randall's spoilt, but I like him, in spite of it. And I like Justin a lot better, now I know him.'

Vanessa looked so delighted that Amanda decided she must be in love with Justin after all. Why this should make her feel worse, she did not know, but her heart sank like a stone. Soon afterwards, they came up with Mr

Deane and Justin, leaning on a gate, having an enjoyable agricultural discussion. When they moved away again, Vanessa took Justin's arm, and the confident, proprietory little gesture sent a sharp stab of jealousy through Amanda. She hated herself for being jealous of Vanessa, but could not help it.

She and her grandfather dropped behind the other two. Mr Deane walked slowly, frequently stopping to look at things. When they reached the bungalow, Vanessa and Justin were only waiting for their return before leaving. Amanda said good-bye with a certain relief. The day had been a little too much for her. She needed time to put on some sort of armour, before she could bear to see Vanessa and Justin together.

She stayed with her grandparents for another week, deliberately prolonging her stay, knowing that they liked having her there. On her last day, she went for a long walk in the hills, now clad in the red and gold splendour of autumn. She could think better out of doors. There was not much of her vacation left, which was a good thing, as she was bound to see Justin sometimes, while she was at home, and would not find it easy to act the part of calm friendship.

When she returned to the university, she determined not to come home again until the Christmas vacation. Work was what she needed, and she was lucky to have work she could still enjoy. She only wished she need not come home at Christmas. The holiday would be filled with preparations for Vanessa's wedding, and to take a cheerful part in it now would demand a self-control like steel.

Amanda passed on to thoughts of her own future. She had never had cut and dried ideas about what she wanted to do, when she had got her degree, but her mind was now made up on one point, at least. She wanted a job that would take her a long way from Northumberland, and Vanessa and

Justin. She could not stay, and witness their life together. A job abroad would be best of all. If she could stay away for three years, she might have managed to cure herself of loving Justin, or at least to accept things as they were. The better the degree she got, the more jobs might be open to her, so that was another good reason for working hard.

When Vanessa came to fetch her the next morning, Amanda strained every nerve to appear cheerful, and to listen with interest to her light-hearted chatter. From various items of news, Vanessa passed on to plans for the remainder of Amanda's vacation. 'I want you to come with me to Northbrook this afternoon, and I'll tell you exactly what we're having done. And then, if the weather's good enough, we'll have a picnic, somewhere on the border; with Justin, of course.'

'But I've been planning to do a fair amount of studying. I'm not going to risk failing my finals.'

'You've never failed an exam yet,'

retorted Vanessa impatiently. 'We've always had a good picnic in the last week of the summer holidays.'

'Oh, all right,' Amanda agreed, resignedly.

After lunch, Vanessa drove her to Northbrook Farm. Work had already begun on some of the alterations, and they wandered around among dust and rubble. 'Right now, it looks a real mess,' said Amanda. 'When do you reckon it will be ready?'

'We're thinking of late January for the wedding, and hope it will be ready by then, so that we can move in as soon as we get back from our honeymoon. It's going to be a lovely house, when it's finished.'

Looking at the work in progress, listening to Vanessa's plans, her marriage seemed to come a long stride nearer. Amanda's heart ached with an intolerable ache, and it was hard work trying to hide her unhappiness behind a mask of gaiety.

Vanessa was out with Justin next day.

Amanda planned to study, but found she could not concentrate. Justin's face, and her own unhappy thoughts kept on coming between her and the printed page. She gave up, and went out for a walk. About a mile from home, she met Randall, out riding. 'It's an age since I've seen you,' he said.

'I've been staying with my grandparents.'

'Oh! Then perhaps you've not heard the latest — the sheep-stealers are at work again. They've lifted twenty of Justin's sheep from Ridley's.'

'I thought they'd left these parts, some time ago.'

'Perhaps they've returned, or perhaps it's another gang. With the present price of meat, it must be quite a profitable racket.'

'You said Justin's sheep,' exclaimed Amanda. 'But I understood he wasn't taking over the farm until next month.'

'The tenant wanted to go earlier, so Justin took it over two weeks ago. He's bought quite a lot of stock, expensive pedigree stock,' added Randall, with relish.

'Well, I think it's pretty mean, that you should sound so pleased at his losing them.'

'If someone's got to suffer from sheep-stealers, I don't see why Justin should get off scot-free. And a fat lot Justin considers me! I told you he wouldn't let Father sell timber, in order to start me up in farming. But now, he's had the almighty cheek to insist that Father should sell that same timber, in order to pay for improvements to some farms. Farms Justin hopes to inherit before long! He doesn't intend me to have a penny from the estate, but he'll see that he feathers his own nest.'

'I think you're being very unfair to Justin,' said Amanda rather hotly.

'Don't tell me you're on his side!' Randall exclaimed, in astonished outrage.

'I'm on the side of the girl who'll be living at Staneshiel. I suppose that *is* the farm you're talking about? Have you seen the inside of the farmhouse?'

'No, but — '

'Well, I have,' interrupted Amanda, 'and I wouldn't want to live in it. I'm on the side of anyone who's prepared to improve that house.'

Randall gave her another look of furious outrage. 'It may interest you to know that Father's absolutely refused. He's told Justin that what he wasn't allowed to sell for his own son, he won't sell for anyone else's benefit.'

He rode off, leaving Amanda wondering what John Roberts would do now — take back his ultimatum, or lose his farm. There seemed nothing Justin could do, especially if his father had taken refuge in ill-health. How he must hate the bitter taste of failure!

When she reached home again, Vanessa had returned, and Amanda heard about the stolen sheep again, from her. 'Justin's talking of going to live at Ridley's,' she said. 'He thinks the farm is particularly vulnerable, if it's known there's no one living there. It seems silly to camp out in one corner of an empty house, and talk about patrolling the hills at night. After all, they've never gone twice to any farm, so Ridley's should be safe enough now.'

'Maybe; but I'd feel pretty mad, if someone stole sheep I'd just bought, at present prices.'

The picnic Vanessa had planned had to be postponed, because of several showery days. Amanda usually knew when Justin was likely to call for Vanessa, or to bring her home, and she kept determinedly out of the way at those times. When she and Vanessa were together, she strained every nerve to appear cheerful, but it was not easy. For once, she found herself counting the days to the end of her vacation, longing to be back at the university, with many miles between herself, and Vanessa and Justin.

Then the clouds rolled away, and Vanessa announced with delight that they would be able to have their picnic, that she had arranged it all with Justin, that he was very busy, but she had insisted that he must spare the time. Amanda listened with very mixed feelings.

Vanessa had arranged that they should take both cars. She would go with Justin, and Amanda could go with them, or with her parents. She went in her father's car. When they arrived at their chosen place, Justin and Vanessa were waiting for them. Vanessa's poodle dashed across to greet Amanda, and she picked him up, finding it easier to move forward and exchange a few words with Justin, with the dog claiming at least part of her attention.

They walked about half a mile to a favourite picnic spot, with a fine view of hills and a river. Amanda saw to it that she was at one end of their half-circle, Justin at the other, but her eyes were irresistibly drawn towards the face she had once thought hard and cold, but which was now so astonishingly dear and familiar. He was sitting beside Vanessa, listening to her animated chatter, a small half-smile on his lips. Amanda hastily withdrew her eyes, and busied herself unpacking a picnic bag.

After lunch, Mr Carr and Justin decided to climb the hill behind them. They invited the two girls to go with them, but both refused, Vanessa from natural indolence, Amanda with uncharacteristic prudence. Some time after they had gone, she said: 'I don't feel like climbing, but I'd rather walk than sit still. What about you, Vanessa?'

'No thanks, but Blackie would love a walk. Take him, and then I'll have more peace.'

Amanda took a footpath along the side of the hill. There was a crisp feel of autumn in the air, and a wind whispering through the heather, but she was conscious only of the unendurable ache in her heart. She knew the path well, and her feet carried her forward automatically, and carried her a good deal farther than she had intended. Coming back to her surroundings with a start, she whistled to Blackie, and retraced her steps, at a faster pace.

She picked up Blackie, to climb some steps in a stone wall. When she reached the top, she saw Justin coming along the path towards her. She subsided on to the wall, and watched him come, feeling suddenly happier than for a long time. It was foolish, but just seeing him so unexpectedly, and the thought of being alone with him, lightened the misery in her heart.

'Vanessa thought you might have got lost,' he greeted her. 'I said that was unlikely, but I'd go and meet you.'

'I only walked farther than I meant.'

Justin leaned against the wall, seeming in no hurry, his eyes on the hills around them. Amanda hugged the poodle against her, and watched him with all her being, not wanting their short time together to end any sooner than it must. 'You've not lost any more sheep?' she asked.

'No. I don't think they'll return to Ridley's. They've usually moved some distance away for their next haul. Of course, it may not be the same gang as before. Just in case, I've moved over to the farmhouse, and do an occasional night patrol along the hills near the road. To my surprise, Randall volunteered to do the same, on alternate nights.'

'Randall!' exclaimed Amanda, in astonishment.

'Yes, Randall,' said Justin, a spark of amusement in his eyes. 'I don't know if he thinks it a lark; or if he hasn't enough to do, and is beginning to get bored. I'm grateful, but expect he'll soon get tired of it.'

'Randall told me your father wouldn't pay for any improvements at Staneshiel,' said Amanda, very hesitantly. 'Is that right?'

The amusement died out of Justin's face, and his mouth set in a bitter line. 'Unfortunately, yes. The family was in an uproar over my proposal to sell timber. My father knows that improvements to Staneshiel are long overdue, and he was willing to agree. But then he talked to Randall about it. He was furious, his mother even more so, and Father isn't well enough to stand being the centre of a family tug-of-war.'

'Has he been really ill?'

'Or just using his health as an excuse to do nothing?' Justin finished her unspoken question, without offence. 'A little of both, I think. He's given in to his family for so long that he finds it difficult now to make a stand, and the fuss did upset him quite badly. But you don't need to worry about John, or Janet. I promised them the house would be improved, so I'll pay for the improvements myself. My grandfather left me some money, and I've some savings from income. I could use it all on equipping Ridley's, but I can't turn it into a first-rate farm, and leave John's to go steadily downhill. I can borrow, if necessary. At least no one will be able to accuse me of trying to feather my own nest at other people's expense.'

It was the very phrase used by Randall, and Amanda wondered how often his family had thrown it in Justin's face. She sat silently looking at his averted face, her heart in her eyes. He turned his head quickly, and hot colour flooded her cheeks. 'Will you take Blackie,' she asked hurriedly, 'and I'll get down. Vanessa will begin to think we're both lost.'

Justin took the dog and put him on the ground, as Amanda scrambled down from the wall. They walked back to the others in complete silence, Amanda racking her brains for something safe to say, finding nothing, and wondering dismally if Justin had realized she was in love with him.

She spent a good deal of the last two days of her vacation finding and packing her belongings, and arguing with Vanessa, who was very indignant about her firmly stated resolve not to come home for any week-ends during the term. 'I don't know why you're making so much fuss. You've got Justin, so you won't be lonely,' said Amanda, somewhat bitterly.

She was rather dismayed to learn that Vanessa had asked Justin to come for tea, on her last day. She could not forget her fear that he might have guessed that she loved him. Things were difficult enough now, trying to pretend that she was entirely happy, when she felt quite the reverse. But if Justin knew, it would be horribly embarrassing for them both.

She lingered upstairs, finishing oddments of packing, tidying her room, until Vanessa came up to fetch her. Justin was sitting talking to her father. Amanda gave him a quick, casual greeting, and a creditably bright smile, slid into her seat, and listened to the conversation. She and Justin had nothing to say to one another, until he got up to go. 'I expect we'll be seeing you some week-end, before long,' he said.

Amanda shook her head, and Vanessa answered for her, very indignantly: 'She says she's not coming home until Christmas, that it'll take her all her time to get through her finals. Such non-sense! Amanda sails through exams. She even *likes* them.'

'I can imagine that. Amanda likes a challenge.' There was a little half-smile in Justin's eyes as he looked at her, and it took all Amanda's self-control to keep her eyes cool and steady, and to hang on to her smile. 'A break does keep you from getting stale,' he added, and then turned quickly back to Vanessa.

Amanda went to bed that night in a state of furious revolt against fate. When she next saw Justin, his marriage to Vanessa would only be a few weeks away. She did not grudge Vanessa her happiness, but she could not help asking how much she had in common with Justin? He was passionately attached to this wild, lonely Northumbrian country, just as Amanda was; but it meant very little to Vanessa. Vanessa was only mildly interested in farming, while love of the land was bred into Justin and Amanda. There was an underlying community of thought and feeling between them. Amanda felt that, in different circumstances, they could have made a very happy life together, with a sharing of warmth and understanding and laughter. But now it could lead to nothing but certain unhappiness for her.

8

Amanda felt a good deal of relief when she was back in Newcastle, away from hurtful associations, and Justin's immediate neighbourhood. She had a bed-sitter in the house of a middle-aged couple, old acquaintances of her father's. She had sometimes thought it might be pleasanter to share with other students, but now the solitude suited her. She no longer had to pretend to be gay, when she was desperately unhappy, and she could go on working, until she was too tired to think.

But no matter how fiercely she concentrated on work, Amanda found that she could not escape from the tyranny of painful thought, nor keep herself from longing for what she could never have. She knew that the things which had made her happy before would make her happy again, but not for some time yet. She had fallen in love with Justin as thoroughly and completely as she did most things, not in any light-hearted fashion, but in a way that would leave a permanent mark on her.

She resisted all suggestions of coming home for a week-end. She needed time, to achieve more command over her thoughts and feelings. Christmas would come all too soon, and she would have to show an eager interest in all Vanessa's wedding preparations. The Easter vacation would be even worse, with Justin and Vanessa married, and settled at Northbrook, expecting her to visit them there. But by the end of the summer term, she ought to have a good degree, and be able to get on with her own life, at a safe distance.

At the beginning of November, a letter from her father told her that her grandfather was ill, and suggested that a visit from her would cheer him up. This was something Amanda could not refuse. She accepted her father's offer to come and fetch her, and consoled herself with the thought that she would be spending most of the week-end at Hesket, so probably would not see Justin at all.

When she reached home on Friday evening, Vanessa gave her an enthusiastic welcome, and a budget of local news, including the fact that Justin had had more sheep stolen, the previous week. 'Again!' exclaimed Amanda. 'They've always said those sheep-rustlers never tried the same farm twice.'

'Justin thinks Ridley's is particularly accessible. There's a lonely unfenced road running for some distance alongside the hill grazing. He and Randall are patrolling near it, on alternate nights. I think it's silly, now the weather's turned so cold. The nights are so long, and they can only be there for a small part of them.'

'True, but I can understand how Justin feels. If I were a farmer, I'd go to almost any lengths to stop those men. It's such a *mean* crime.'

Vanessa had put her car at Amanda's disposal, so she drove over to Hesket, after breakfast next morning. She found her grandfather not very ill, but uncommonly depressed. He was unused to illness, and hated having to be indoors, and inactive. After a little of Amanda's company, he perked up considerably. She was his favourite grandchild, partly because she reminded him of her mother, and partly because they were rather alike. She talked to him about her life in Newcastle, and retailed Vanessa's news and gossip of the night before, and he became quite cheerful. She divided her time between talking to him, and helping her grandmother, and stayed late, knowing that she only had two days at home. It was a little after ten o'clock when she left, promising to return next day.

The night was dark and cloudy, with a thin drizzle falling. Because she knew she was rather inexperienced, Amanda was a very careful driver, her normal impulsiveness held firmly in check. On this dark, misty night, she drove even more slowly than usual. Near home, she slowed to a crawl, as a van turned right, across her path. She drove on a few yards, then put her foot down hard on the brake. She sat staring into the darkness, a small frown puckering her forehead, Going over the cross-roads, she had instinctively glanced down the lane, after the van, and seen nothing, only black darkness. It had taken several seconds for the strangeness of this to register on her mind. She should have seen the van's tail-lights. This being home ground, she knew that the lane ran straight for some distance. The van had gone into the lane only seconds before, moving slowly for the turn, and could not possibly have reached the first bend. The drizzle was thick, but not as thick as that. No, the only possible conclusion was that the van's rear lights were out. And Amanda could have sworn that they were on, when the van turned across her path. Why had they switched the lights off, immediately they turned down that lane?

Inevitably, her mind turned to sheep-rustlers, and the various things she had heard about them — a professional gang, operating fairly near a road, on a dark, moonless night like this, with a van big enough to hold a number of sheep. That lane ran for a short distance between hedged fields, then became an unfenced road winding through hills, and on one side those hills belonged to Ridley's Farm.

Commonsense told Amanda that she ought to drive home as quickly as possible, and ring up the police and Justin. But the gang could have collected a load of sheep, and driven off, before anyone arrived on the scene. If the van was a perfectly innocent one, she would feel a fool. She glanced at the shelf, where a torch was always kept, and her eyes fell on her camera. She had taken a photograph of her grandmother in her kitchen, put in a flash-bulb, intending to take a second picture, and then the telephone had rung, and the picture had not been taken. Amanda stared at the camera, thinking that if she could find the sheep-stealers in the act, she might get a flashlight photograph, which could eventually catch them.

Commonsense retired defeated, and her natural impetuosity took command. She switched off the engine, pocketed the camera, got out, and locked the car. How much she was influenced by the thought that Justin might be in danger of losing more sheep, she did not pause to ask herself. Neither could she be certain that a photograph, taken under such conditions, would be worth having. But the camera had been Vanessa's birthday present, and was a very expensive one.

She decided to go through the fields, parallel with the lane, so climbed the dry-stone wall, switched on her torch, and hurried forward at a stumbling run, crossing three fields, and three more walls. Then she was out on the open hillside. Switching off the torch, she stood still, trying to get her bearings. It was very dark, but a wind blowing across the hills had blown away most of the mist. She could just make out the lighter surface of the road, and moved cautiously towards it, her eyes growing accustomed to the darkness. A dark shape loomed up, and she realized that it was the van, parked at the side of the road. She paused, thinking hard. Could she do anything to the van, to immobilize it? She didn't really know enough about engines, and a man might have remained with the van. Belatedly, Amanda decided that she ought to have gone for help, but it was too late for that. She must just do what she could, alone.

She moved noiselessly forward, wondering if it would be worth trying to get a photograph of the van. Then she was brought to a full stop by a sudden commotion farther up the hill, sheep baa-ing in a very agitated fashion. Definitely sheep-stealers at work, she thought, and decided not to risk going right up to the van. It would be better to wait fairly near it, in some sort of cover. It was bound to take time to get a load of protesting sheep into the van, so she might be able to get a good look at the men, and perhaps take a photograph as well.

Before she had gone half the distance to the road, all hell seemed to break loose on the hill above her. There was a burst of furious barking, the sound of men's raised voices, then an anguished howl of pain, followed by the sharp, unmistakable sound of a shot. Amanda froze in her tracks, scared for the first time that night. The brief silence that followed the shot was broken by the sound of running feet, and then a second shot echoed around the hills. Amanda realized that the feet were pounding towards her, that she was directly between the men and their van. Fear suddenly left her. Pulling the camera from her pocket, she stepped behind a clump of gorse bushes, and waited. Two running figures appeared in the darkness. Amanda stepped quickly out of her shelter, and the night was lit by a blinding flash, as she pressed the trigger. The feet came to an abrupt halt. There was a startled exclamation. But Amanda was already away, flying for her life, up the hill.

She ran in the direction from which the commotion seemed to have come, stumbling and almost falling on the rough ground, but not daring to use her torch. Then, above the pounding of her own heart, she heard the sound of an engine starting up. She stopped to listen, and then, near at hand, she heard another sound, part growl, part bark, and part whimper. She switched on her torch, and saw a dog, only a few feet away. He was half-sitting, half-lying. With a sickening lurch of fear, Amanda recognized him as Justin's Labrador.

She moved cautiously towards him, saying: 'Bruno, you know me, don't you?' She thought the dog knew her, although they had only met once. He stopped growling, and got to his feet, and Amanda saw a trickle of blood on his golden coat. That must have been one of the shots she had heard, but who had stopped the other?

The dog began to move slowly, limpingly uphill, looking at her as though telling her to follow. Amanda needed no telling. She kept pace with him, the torch in her hand. Then Bruno broke into a limping run, and she saw a dark mound ahead of them. There was a startled exclamation, and part of the mound detached itself, and stood up. A second later, Amanda recognized Randall. 'You!' she exclaimed, and then her eyes went to the prone figure over which he had been stooping, and she dropped to her knees beside it. 'Justin! Did they shoot him?' The dog snuffled at Justin's face, but he did not move. 'Is he badly hurt?' demanded Amanda, frantic with fear for him.

'I don't know. There was a shot, and he went down like a ninepin. Then they made off. It's too dark to see how badly he's hurt, and I'm afraid to move him. What shall we do?'

Randall sounded completely unnerved

and frightened. Strangely enough, the panic in his voice had a steadying effect on Amanda, perhaps because she realized that it was no use expecting him to take charge. 'Shine my torch on him, while I have a look,' she told him, wishing she knew even a little about first-aid. She could see no mark on Justin's face, so she unbuttoned his sheepskin jacket, and slid her hand inside. She could feel his heart beating, and, she thought, quite strongly. She pulled the jacket back into place, and sat back on her heels, white and frightened, but still practical. 'I can't see where he's hurt, but he's alive, and it may not be much. We'll have to have help. You could go quicker than me. I left Vanessa's car by the cross-roads, about three-quarters of a mile away. Which would be the quickest way to a telephone, to go down to Ridley's, or to get the car?'

'The car. I could run along the road, but not over this rough ground in the dark.'

'Here's the key then. Get to the

nearest telephone, and ring for an ambulance. Tell them they'll have to carry a man over rough ground. Then collect some rugs or blankets, and come back here.' She told Randall exactly where to find the car. As he turned away, she added: 'Give me your coat. You can keep yourself warm, but Justin can't.'

Randall pulled off his coat, and dropped it beside her. 'There's a whisky flask in the pocket,' he said, and then she heard his feet running down the hill. She turned back to Justin, cold fear at her heart, and put Randall's coat over him, tucking it in, wishing there was something more she could do, and furious at her own ignorance. Justin's head was lying on an outcrop of rock, and it looked dreadfully uncomfortable. Although it might be safer, and although he was unconscious, Amanda could not bear to leave it like that. She pulled off her scarf, folded it, and eased it gently beneath his head. Her fingers encountered something sticky, and a wave of sickening fear flowed over her. Had Justin been

215

shot through the head? A moment later, she realized that he might easily have cut his head, falling on that rock. But even that could be pretty bad.

There was no sound in all the silent night, except Justin's quick, shallow breathing, the dog panting beside him, and the melancholy whine of the wind. Amanda felt for Justin's pulse. Even with the addition of Randall's coat, his hand felt icy cold. She pulled off her own coat, added that, and then waited, while each minute seemed to drag itself out into hours, filled with dread and uncertainty. Her teeth began to chatter, and before long she felt as though her very bones were chattering. She would not risk trying to give Justin any whisky, but now she fished Randall's flask from the pocket, and took a good swig herself, gasped, and felt a warm glow travelling through her. Under its stimulus, she realized that, if she got underneath Justin's coverings, she could keep him warmer, and might even be a bit warmer herself.

She eased herself gently beneath the coats. They still left most of her uncovered, and the damp cold of the ground bit into her bones. She wondered what it was doing to Justin, and moved one hand to feel his face gently. He stirred beneath her touch, and muttered: 'Randall.'

Amanda sat up on one elbow, gazing down at him. 'Not Randall, Amanda,' she said softly but clearly, and switched on her torch, holding it to the side of his face, so that it should not dazzle him.

Justin's eyes were open. They stared up at her, looking black in the torchlight. 'Amanda!' he said, in a voice of total bewilderment.

'Randall's gone for help. He'll be back soon. Are you in pain?' But Justin's eyes shut again, and his brief flash of consciousness flickered out. Amanda looked down at him, fear clutching at her heart. Was he badly hurt? Perhaps bleeding from some wound, while she sat helplessly by? But, better to do nothing than to do the wrong thing. She leaned over him, listening to his quick breathing. 'If only I knew what to do!' she said aloud. 'Oh, Justin, don't die, darling, don't die!'

She didn't know how long it was since Randall had left them, but it seemed a very long time. Then, a few minutes later, she saw car lights travelling along the road. They stopped. Amanda got to her feet, and shone her torch. Minutes passed, and then Randall came panting up the hill, a roll of blankets under his arm. Amanda took them, and tucked them around Justin. 'The ambulance is on its way,' said Randall, getting his breath. 'I left the car lights on, so they'd see where to stop. How is he?'

'I don't know. He came round for a few seconds, but then went right out again.'

Randall stood gazing down at his brother. Then he glanced at Amanda. 'Where's your coat?'

'Over Justin. He felt terribly cold.'

'You must be perished. Have this.' Randall pulled off the coat he was wearing, and put it round Amanda. 'I've plenty on underneath, and it's your father's coat anyway. I went there to telephone, and he insisted on my taking his coat. Look, lights down on the road. Give me your torch, and I'll guide them up here.'

Very soon, lights came bobbing up the hill, and two large men appeared, carrying powerful torches and a stretcher. Amanda grabbed Bruno, who seemed inclined to resent these strangers. The men bent over Justin. 'Can't do anything here. We'll have to move him. You two shine the torches, while we get him on the stretcher.'

The dog objected strenuously to this, especially when Justin gave one sharp cry. Amanda held him with one hand, the torch in the other. When they began to move downhill, Bruno seemed reassured, and she was able to let go of him. Randall helped with the stretcher. Amanda lit the way, and Bruno trotted behind. When they reached the ambulance, she looked at Randall. 'I suppose you'll go with him?'

'I'd much rather you did,' he answered promptly. 'Though I really don't see why you should.'

'I don't mind,' said Amanda, who was longing to go with Justin. 'You take Vanessa's car, and the dog. He's hurt too, but I don't think badly.'

'I'll take him home, let your people know that you've stayed with Justin, and then follow you to the hospital.'

Amanda got into the ambulance, and could see Justin clearly at last. His eyes were shut, and he moved his head restlessly, muttering inaudibly. She thought he looked dreadfully ill. Sliding her hand beneath the covers, she felt for his cold hand, and held it tightly in hers. Once, during the journey, his eyes flickered open, and looked straight up into hers. Amanda instinctively murmured endearing reassurances, regardless of the attendant. After a few seconds Justin's eyelids drooped over his eyes again, and he lay without moving.

At the hospital, Justin was whisked

way, and Amanda was taken to a waiting-room. 'You don't look too good yourself,' said the young nurse. 'Anything wrong with you?'

'Only cold, after sitting on a cold, open hillside.'

'I'll get you a hot drink.'

Between the warm room and the coffee, Amanda soon began to thaw, but the minutes dragged by on leaden feet, while she waited for news, and wondered what was happening to Justin. It was a relief when Randall joined her. 'Any news?' he asked. Amanda shook her head silently, and he sat down beside her. 'I told your people I'd drive you home, but I didn't know what time it might be.'

'Has Vanessa been told about Justin?'

'Oh, yes. She asked if she should come with me, but I told her there was no point in that. She wouldn't be able to see Justin, and we'd let her know as soon as we hear anything ourselves. I've told Mother, but she'll keep it from Father, for the time being. That should be easier, as Justin's been over at Ridley's most of the time.'

Randall spoke in nervous jerks, looking about as frightened and worried as Amanda felt. Even at that moment, she was surprised by this, after the way Randall had talked about his brother. She felt that he must have more affection for Justin than he had ever shown, and her heart warmed to him. 'I shall stay until I know how Justin is, but there's no need for you to stay. Would you rather I ran you home now?' he asked.

'I'd much rather stay, until we hear some news.'

'Good. I'd *hate* to have to sit here alone, wondering.'

'I don't think he's very badly hurt,' said Amanda, trying to reassure herself, as well as Randall. 'And he's pretty tough and fit.'

'If he is badly hurt, I'll never forgive myself. It was all my fault.'

'Nonsense! How could it be your fault? You didn't shoot him,' retorted

Amanda bracingly. She looked at Randall's white, tense face, and an odd little detail suddenly crossed her mind. 'Justin said that you and he went round the hills on alternate nights. Why were you together, tonight?'

'We weren't together. It was my night to be on patrol. I thought Justin was out with Vanessa. I don't know why he was there. Unless he suspected something.'

'Suspected what, for goodness sake?' demanded Amanda, impatiently, unable to make sense of these disjointed remarks.

'That I was helping those men to steal his sheep,' said Randall.

Amanda stared at him, completely bereft of speech. Then horrified comprehension dawned in her eyes. 'You were in with those *sheep-stealers?*'

Randall looked back at her, silently, guiltily. Then the door opened, and a nurse came in. They jumped to their feet, only one thought in both their minds. She smiled reassuringly, and spoke to Randall. 'Your brother's not badly hurt.

He was shot through the right shoulder. The bone is broken, and he has concussion, and a nasty cut on the head, where he fell; but he's in no danger. You can go home now, if you like; or wait and talk to the doctor when he's free.'

'We'll wait,' they answered, in unison.

Something seemed to have gone wrong with Amanda's legs. She sat down very abruptly. Then she looked at Randall. He was sitting with his face buried in his hands, his shoulders shaking uncontrollably, and Amanda realized that he had been under an even worse strain than herself. Jumping to her feet, she put her arm round his shoulders, and gave him an affectionate, impulsive hug. 'He's going to be all right, Randall. And it wasn't all your fault.'

'I know now how it feels to be a murderer.'

'Stop being melodramatic. You didn't fire the shot, and I don't expect you knew the men had guns.'

'Of course, I didn't.' Amanda's

bracing commonsense had a steadying effect on Randall. He made a great effort to pull himself together. 'You're a good sort, Amanda; but you must think me a complete worm.'

'I think you've been an utter fool,' she told him candidly. 'But the really important thing is that Justin's going to be all right.' Randall gave her a fleeting, curious glance, but said nothing. Amanda returned to her chair, and sat thinking over what Randall had just told her. 'Why did you do it? Do you really hate Justin?' she asked.

'I thought I did,' he answered slowly. 'He's never been quite one of us, and never wanted to be. When we were kids, he was forever throwing it in my face that Danesford would be his, one day, and never mine. We never got on. Then, after he took charge of things up here, he wanted to be absolute dictator, tell everyone what they could or could not do. And everything I wanted, he vetoed.'

'But Randall, did you never realize

that Justin was bound to feel the odd one out, in some ways? His mother was dead, and your mother would have preferred you to be the heir. Did any of you *try* to make him feel that he belonged as completely as you and Caroline? Did you never think that he chucked Danesford in your face, because it was the one thing in which he did come first? That it helped to balance the fact that you were the favourite with both your parents?'

'No, I can't say I did. But perhaps you're right,' he answered, in honest surprise.

If Justin had been in danger, Amanda might have been unable to forgive Randall. But she knew that he was horrified and ashamed of what he had done, and she had always liked him, even when she most disapproved of him. 'Well, let's just be thankful the damage is no worse,' she said. She looked at her watch, thinking they had been waiting a good while for the doctor, and beginning to wonder if anything could have gone wrong. She suddenly found herself shivering uncontrollably.

'What's wrong? Are you cold?' asked Randall.

'No; just scared.'

'Me, too.' Randall moved his chair close to Amanda's and put one arm about her shoulders, drawing her against him, and she took comfort from the knowledge that he was as concerned about Justin as she was. They sat silently together, until the door opened again. This time it was the doctor. 'Your brother will be all right,' he told Randall. 'He has a broken shoulder bone, concussion and shock, and he's lost quite a bit of blood, but he's young, and tough. He'll soon be as good as new.' Turning to Amanda, he added: 'You should be able to see him for a short time tomorrow, or the next day.' She realized that he took her for Justin's fiancée, or girl-friend. A faint colour came into her white face, but she said nothing.

She got into her coat, which had

been returned to her some time earlier, and she and Randall went out into the darkness. They drove in silence, until Randall stopped at the cottage. Then Amanda said: 'Keep Vanessa's car to get home in, Randall. You can return it sometime tomorrow.'

'Well, it would be quicker. Thanks. And for everything else. I don't know what I'd have done without you.'

As Amanda got out of the car, the front door opened, and her father came down the path to meet her. He drew her indoors, to the sitting-room. Vanessa was sitting by the fire, in a house-coat, looking white and very anxious. Amanda could only look at her, silently. Vanessa jumped to her feet, asking impatiently: 'What's been happening? How is Justin?'

'He's all right; he's not badly hurt,' said Amanda, finding her tongue. 'I ought to have rung you up from the hospital, but I must have been too tired to think straight.'

'You look all in.' Her father firmly

steered her into a chair. 'I'll get some coffee. Don't bother her with questions yet, Vanessa. Justin's all right, so wait for the details.'

Amanda looked at Vanessa's pale, strained face, and thought: 'So she does love Justin.' Although she ached with weariness, she pulled herself together, and repeated what the doctor and nurse had told them.

'But how did you come into it, in the first place?' demanded Vanessa. At that moment Mr Carr reappeared, with coffee for everyone. Amanda thankfully postponed explanations.

She drank her coffee, and then gave them a brief account of the night's events. But she said nothing about Randall's disclosures. 'You should have come home, and rung the police,' said her father.

'It probably would have been more sense,' Amanda admitted. 'But I'm glad I didn't. The men would have been miles away before the police could get there, and I don't know what Randall would have done alone. He had to get help, yet wouldn't have wanted to have left Justin there alone.'

'You took a crazy risk, even if it did turn out well,' said Mr Carr. 'Bed for the pair of you, now; and don't get up early. I'll ring up the hospital, first thing, and come and tell you what they say.'

They went upstairs, and Amanda began to undress, with slow mechanical movements. As she hung up her coat, she felt the camera, weighing it down. She had forgotten it in the press of later events. She pulled it out, and stood, turning it over in her hands. That flashlight photograph might be a dud, or a valuable piece of evidence. She would have to give the film to the police.

She got into bed, but could not sleep. A vivid procession of the night's events streamed through her tired mind. When she finally began to slide towards sleep, a sudden thought jerked her wide-awake. If she gave the film to the police, and it helped them to trace the sheep-stealers, Randall's part in the affair was bound to come out. The whole country-side would learn that he had been helping to steal his brother's sheep. What a scandal! Justin would probably hate it as much as Randall. She simply could not do that to them. But would it be fair to suppress the film? If the men went undetected, they might continue to prey on local farmers, men like John Roberts, who could ill afford to lose stock. And if they went about the work carrying guns, someone else might get shot. It seemed to Amanda that she had no choice, that she must be on the side of the law. Then she thought of Mr Warren. In his precarious state of health, Justin's accident would be a bad enough shock, without his having to learn about Randall's part in it, and to know that all their family disagreements and bitterness were exposed to public gaze.

It was an appalling problem, which Amanda considered from every angle, without reaching any firm decision. She drifted into a brief, uneasy sleep, and woke to hear her father coming upstairs. She jumped out of bed, and flung a dressing-gown round her. He went to Vanessa's room, assuming that she was the most anxious for news. Amanda followed, to hear him saying: 'They say his condition is very satisfactory, and he can have one visitor this afternoon, for a very short time. Vanessa, of course.'

'Of course,' agreed Amanda, and went quickly back to her own room, wishing she did not so fiercely resent Vanessa's right to be Justin's first visitor. She longed to see him, to reassure herself, and to ask him what she ought to do about that film. She knew he would not want his brother exposed, or his father upset, but he would think about other farmers. Amanda would have been guided by his wishes, if only she could have talked to him.

Telling herself that Justin was probably not fit to be worried by her problem, Amanda got dressed. She decided that she must talk to Randall, before she *did* anything. He would have to bring Vanessa's car back, sometime, but it might be difficult to have any private conversation. Neither could she discuss such a thing over the telephone. She decided she would have to walk down to Danesford, as soon as breakfast was over. She went down, and Mrs Carr embarked on a flood of questions. Amanda answered, rather briefly, and then her father came to her rescue, saying: 'Let her eat in peace. She looks as though she hasn't slept a wink, and I'm sure she doesn't want to go over it all again.'

Amanda gave him a very grateful look, and had nearly finished her breakfast when Vanessa appeared. She looked as though she hadn't slept much, either. When Amanda stated her intention of going to see Randall, there was an unexpected outcry from her parents. 'After being up half the night, and sitting on a cold hillside, you can just stay at home today, and take things easy,' said Mrs Carr. 'If it won't wait until Randall returns

Vanessa's car, then ring him up.'

'It wouldn't do. Mr Warren has not been told about Justin's accident, and he might overhear something,' Amanda told her, knowing that it sounded rather weak.

Mr Carr sighed. 'If you're hell-bent on going, I'll run you there. You can drive yourself back, in Vanessa's car.'

When she arrived at Danesford, she was told that Randall was out at the stables. She found him just starting up Vanessa's car. He looked very astonished at seeing her. 'What brings you here? I was just coming up to your place, with this car.'

'I've got to talk to you, and it would be difficult at home, with everyone around.'

'I wouldn't mind talking to you,' he admitted. 'We can be private enough up here,' and he took her to a small room above the stables.

'Have you told anyone that you were helping those sheep-stealers?' asked Amanda.

'No, I have not.' Randall hesitated. 'Did you tell your family?'

'No, not about that. But, Randall, I took a photograph of those two men.'

'A photograph!'

'I happened to have the camera with me. It's a very good one. Vanessa gave it to me for my birthday. So I took it with me, and when the two men came running right past me, I took a flashlight photograph. It may not be any good, but I think I ought to give it to the police.'

Randall looked at her in silence for a long minute. 'Have you thought what it could do to my father, if everything became public?'

'Of course I have. That's why I wanted to talk to you, before doing anything. I don't want to make trouble for you, or your father, but sheep-stealing is everyone's business. If those men usually carry guns, someone may be killed, and if I'd kept evidence to myself, I'd be partly to blame. I wish I could talk to Justin, and find out what he thinks.'

'He'd be perfectly justified in turning me over to the police, but he'll consider the effect on Father.'

'Yes; but he'll think about all the other farmers in the district, as well.'

'I don't know if it makes any difference to you,' said Randall slowly, 'but that pair last night are not part of the gang who lifted sheep from so many farms, during the summer. That lot left this district weeks ago. Oh, I can't swear to that. It's only gossip from shady characters on racecourses, but I think they knew what they were talking about. And that's what last night's pair were, a couple of shady characters I'd met at race meetings. They told me they knew exactly how much those earlier thieves made, and where they sold the sheep, and said they wished they could make money so easily. That's what put the idea into my head.'

He glanced at Amanda's expressive face, coloured, but went doggedly on: 'I told them that, if they provided transport, I'd provide the sheep, and see that no one was around. I arranged for them to come on a night when I was doing night patrol, and Justin was at a farmers meeting, on the other side of the county. I bought a sheep-dog from a friend, rounded up some sheep, as soon as Justin was clear away, and fastened them in an old sheep-fold. I arranged to meet those two on the road, and took them up to the sheep-fold. I arranged to meet them again last night, believing that Justin was taking Vanessa over to the coast, for an evening out. But I think he must have smelt a rat, and told me that to tempt me, because he was up there, waiting near the sheep-fold. I don't know what he planned to do, but that dog of his went berserk, and flew at one of the men. And then everything seemed to happen in a split second.' He looked up, and met Amanda's eyes again. 'I can see what you think of me, but it can't be worse than what I think of myself. I suppose I've always been jealous of Justin, because he was the eldest, and would inherit Danesford.

But all that time we waited in the hospital, I kept on thinking that, if he died, Danesford would be mine one day, and that it would be quite unbearable to inherit it that way. I can tell you, I'll never covet Danesford again.'

Randall's voice broke, and he buried his face in his hands. It was obvious to Amanda that he was still badly shocked, and she could not be harsh. 'I doubt if you quite realized what you were doing,' she said slowly. 'But, Randall, why can't you grow up? If these men are not regular sheep-stealers, it does make a difference. Only, can you be sure they won't go on to steal from other farms?'

'Not they! They wouldn't know how to round up sheep, and no other farmer would do the job for them. And they must have had quite a fright.'

'But they may talk. They know you, and may blackmail you.'

'Talk might land them in the dock, on a charge of carrying guns without a licence, and shooting Justin. They'll keep quiet, in their own interest. And I think I'd rather chance being black-mailed than — ' Randall broke off abruptly, as a new thought came into his mind. 'You photographed them! D'you think they realized it?'

'They saw the flash, and stopped. But I was off and away up the hill, before they could do anything.'

'You're a cool one, I must say, to think of such a thing,' said Randall, admiringly. 'If I tell those two that an outsider has a photograph of them, and will give it to the police, if there's the least hint of blackmail, or taking sheep from any other farm, that should keep them quiet.'

'It's a pity you don't use your wits for something better,' Amanda commented, somewhat scathingly. 'If there's no danger to anyone else, I'll go on keeping quiet about it, at least until I know what Justin means to do. My family assumed that you and Justin were together, and they can continue to think that. Well, I might as well take Vanessa's car home, and save you the trouble.'

'Would you mind if I came with you? As Justin can have one visitor, I suppose Vanessa will go this afternoon, and I wondered if I could go with her. We've not told Father about Justin yet. Mother thought it would worry him less, if we could tell him that Vanessa had seen him, and thought he didn't seem too bad. She might come back to Danesford, and talk to Father herself.'

'Come by all means, if you don't mind walking home.'

'I'm not coming back here. I'll go over to Ridley's, and see what needs doing there. I do know what I'm about on a farm, and it seems the least I can do.'

They drove back to the cottage, and went in together. Randall made his request, to which Vanessa readily agreed. Then he turned to Mr Carr. 'I want you to know that we all feel deeply in Amanda's debt. She kept her head last night, when I'd gone to pieces, and put her coat over Justin, to keep him warm, while she sat and froze in the bitter wind.'

'Anyone would have done as much!'

exclaimed Amanda, her face on fire, yet oddly touched by such a generous tribute from Randall.

When he had gone, her father looked at her thoughtfully: 'Randall seems to have a very high opinion of you. I won't quarrel with that, but I hope there's no kind of attachment? He's charming, but — '

'Much too young for his age. Don't worry. There's nothing like that,' Amanda assured him, thinking she would rather be suspected of that, than of the real truth.

A couple of hours later, there was a ring at the door, and her father told her that a policeman wanted to see her. Amanda was very startled, but then realized that gun-shot wounds in the night could hardly go unexplained. She answered all his questions quite frankly, but still felt uneasy and oddly guilty about keeping back any mention of her camera.

She told Randall about the policeman's visit, when he returned that afternoon. 'He came to see me too,' he said. 'I told him that Justin and I went out together, and that it was too dark to see the men's faces. That part of it was true. Don't worry. They'll lie low, and we'll hear no more about it.'

He and Vanessa drove away together. Amanda had rung up her grandmother, to say that she would be unable to come that day, because of being up most of the night. So now she had no occupation, and could only sit by the fire, pretending to read, and wishing with all her heart that she could have gone to see Justin, instead of Vanessa.

Vanessa had agreed to go on to Danesford for tea, and to tell Mr Warren about her visit to the hospital, so it was a good while before she returned. She still looked very pale and anxious. 'Justin says he feels fine, except for a headache, but I think he looks awful,' she told them. 'Actually, I only had a few minutes with him. He'd been demanding to see Randall, and got in such a state that they said it would be better to let him have his way, but rationed us both for time. Randall said he wanted to give him some instructions about the farm.' It was easy for Amanda to guess that Justin had a much more urgent reason than this. But she was silent, watching Vanessa, who was biting her lip, as though trying not to cry. 'The nurse said he'd lost a lot of blood, and was still suffering from shock and concussion, but would probably look a lot better tomorrow. I shall go again, in the afternoon, and he asked me to bring you, so that he can thank you himself.'

'I don't need thanks,' exclaimed Amanda. 'And I meant to go back to Newcastle, first thing, tomorrow.'

'Surely you can stay one more day? Justin seemed very anxious to see you.'

'Oh, well, I suppose I can,' said Amanda. Perhaps Justin did not wholly trust Randall's assurances of her silence, and wanted to hear it from her, too. In that case, it would be ungenerous to refuse. After envying Vanessa the privilege of seeing Justin, it was quite illogical to feel, now, that she did not want to see him. But Amanda had suddenly begun to remember the endearments she had spoken, when she had believed Justin was unconscious. He had come round quite suddenly, twice. Suppose he had been somewhere on the borderline between consciousness and unconsciousness, had heard her words, and remembered them? It was a very disquieting thought.

Having agreed to stay another day, Amanda drove to Hesket next morning, and gave her grandfather a firsthand, but not quite complete, account of the affair. After lunch, she and Vanessa drove to the hospital. Justin was in a private room, Vanessa told her. He was only allowed one visitor at a time, so perhaps Amanda had better go first.

Amanda followed her directions, and arrived at the door, her heart hammering on her ribs. She took a deep breath, and went in. After one quick look at Justin, a smile lit her eyes. 'You look much better than I expected.'

'I suppose that's Vanessa. She seemed determined I was at death's door,' he answered, with a wry grin.

Amanda stood looking down at him, agitation, pain, and pleasure mingling in her heart. Justin's face was always thin. It was now very pale, and heavily bandaged, but his eyes looked very much alive. 'Vanessa told me you wanted to see me,' she said. 'I don't want thanks, Justin; and if it's about Randall — ' her voice hesitated. She was not quite certain how much he knew.

'Do sit down, Amanda, and then I can see you more comfortably. Randall's told me everything. He says you know it all, and have promised to say nothing. I'd do almost anything to keep it from my father.'

'I know. And I've no wish to make trouble for Randall, either. I think it's taught him quite a lot.'

'Yesterday, I thought he'd grown up overnight,' said Justin soberly. Then added with a grin: 'And not before time, either. I don't want you to think the ill-feeling between us was all his fault. I was to blame, too. I always felt that Randall was the favourite, then Caroline; and I came last. But where Danesford was concerned, I came first, so I never let him forget it. When he got whatever he wanted, and crowed over me, I used to retaliate that Danesford was one thing he could never have, and I wouldn't have him there, when it was mine. Kid's stuff, but there was enough truth in it to poison our relationship, especially when Randall's mother encouraged him to believe he had a right to anything he wanted. And recent money difficulties haven't improved things.'

'Did you know it was Randall?'

'No; but small things added up to a very strong suspicion. That sheep-dog, the fact that someone seemed to know a good deal about my movements, and all the droppings in that fold, which proved that sheep had been penned there, beforehand. I couldn't accuse Randall on mere suspicion. I had to make sure.

But what I would like to know, is how you came to be there? When I came round, I had a vague recollection of your being there, but it seemed so unlikely I thought I must have dreamt it, until Randall told me it was true.'

Amanda listened with very mixed feelings, wondering if he remembered any of her unthinking words, but Justin's face was never easy to read. She told him about the van, and her decision to investigate, and what followed. He listened in silence, then asked: 'Didn't you give a thought to the danger?'

'There wasn't time. Everything happened too quickly. And it was easy to get away in the dark. I'm glad I didn't stop to think. Randall wouldn't have known what to do, alone. He was completely bowled over by the result of his own actions.'

Justin gave her a quick glance, and Amanda found herself wondering if he, like her father, suspected her of defending Randall because she was in love with him. All he said was: 'Will you get the photograph developed, and keep it, if it's any good? We'd have to give it to the police, if other sheep were stolen.'

His voice sounded suddenly tired, so Amanda got quickly to her feet. 'Vanessa's waiting to see you, so I must go.'

Justin's left hand came out, and gripped one of hers, with surprising strength. 'You say you don't want thanks, Amanda, so I'll only say that you're a gift to anyone in a jam.'

She stood for a few moments looking down at him with almost unbearable love and tenderness, then turned quickly away, unable to say anything. She went down to where Vanessa was waiting, and then went out to sit in the car. She was reassured by Justin's looks, but overwhelmed by the intensity of the longing that shook her. Out there on the hills, in the night, in spite of all her fears, she had felt closer to him than ever before. And they would never be as close again, she told herself. She loved him beyond measure, and she could not stay to watch his life with Vanessa. She must get away from here, and find something to fill the aching hollow inside her.

It was not long before Vanessa came out. Amanda sat up, and tried to look cheerful. Vanessa looked very subdued. She stopped by Amanda's window, and asked: 'Would you mind driving back?'

'If you like.' Amanda slid over to the driving seat, and studied her step-sister's face, as she got in. 'What's wrong?'

'I thought Justin looked terrible, didn't you?'

'No; I thought he looked a lot better than I expected. Pale, of course, but remarkably lively, all things considered.'

Vanessa still looked miserable. Although she did not make an undue fuss when she was ill, Amanda knew that Vanessa was always scared, when others were ill. Amanda believed this was a reaction from her father's illness and death, when she was a child, and was usually sympathetic. But for once, she was feeling too sorry for herself to have much sympathy left over for Vanessa's lesser worries. They drove home in silence.

9

Amanda went back to the university next morning, but found it very difficult to keep her mind on her work. She rang her home several times, and each time was told that Justin was making a good recovery. At the last moment, she agreed to Vanessa's suggestion of a week-end at home. Justin was still in hospital, so she need not fear an encounter with him, and she would like to see her grandfather again. She went by bus to Thurston, and found Randall waiting for her, not Vanessa as she had expected. 'Vanessa told me you were coming,' he explained. 'I asked if I could come and meet you, because it seemed a good chance for a talk.'

'How's everyone, including Justin?'

'He's getting on fine, thank goodness. My father's not too grand. He was badly shaken by Justin's accident. I

251

don't know what might have happened, if he'd had to hear the whole story. So far, the police have been unable to trace the two men, but I managed to have a word with them, and told them about the photograph. Believe me, they'll give sheep a wide berth for the future. Justin and I are both deeply grateful to you, for everything.'

Amanda made a gesture of disclaimer. 'When will Justin be out of hospital?'

'Not for a week or two yet. He'd rather not go to Danesford, because they're in the thick of preparations for Caroline's wedding, but he can't go to Ridley's on his own. I thought I'd move over there, and do what I could to help.'

'That *would* be a change.'

Randall grinned back at her. 'Tell you the truth, I'm pretty sick of the wedding turmoil. Father isn't well enough to give Caro away. Justin's got a perfect excuse, so I've been landed with the job, *and* making a speech afterwards. Seriously though, you'd be surprised how much better Justin and I get on.

I've been looking after Ridley's, and acting as his messenger boy around the estate. I've learnt a lot in a week, and must admit Justin's got good reason for demanding economy.'

'That's a very generous admission.'

'Oh, I'm a reformed character,' declared Randall with a little grin of self-mockery, and Amanda thought that at least one good thing seemed to have come out of the sorry affair. If Justin and Randall could at last be friends, that would be one problem less for Justin. She went indoors feeling considerably cheered. Vanessa told her that Justin was much better, but she still looked worried and nervy.

Amanda borrowed Vanessa's car, next morning, and drove over to see her grandfather, who was also much better. She returned for lunch, so that Vanessa could have the car for her afternoon visit to Justin. About an hour after Vanessa had gone, Mr and Mrs Carr left, to spend the rest of the day with friends, so Amanda was left alone, with only her thoughts for company. They were not very good company.

It was nearly five when Vanessa returned. Amanda enquired after Justin. 'Oh, he's up, and looking quite a lot better.'

'Then why do you keep on looking so careworn?' demanded Amanda, with a touch of impatience.

Vanessa pushed back her dark hair, with a harassed gesture. 'I'm no good with sick people. I just don't know how to talk to them, and it makes me feel so inadequate.'

'I should know that,' returned Amanda, with a faint grin. 'You act scared, even with me, on the few occasions I've been ill. But surely it's easier, now that Justin is so much better?'

'I hate the atmosphere of a hospital. I'll be all right, once he's out.'

Vanessa drifted off upstairs, and Amanda made the tea. After they had cleared it away, they settled down to read, but Amanda could not fix her mind on her book. Her eyes would keep on straying to Vanessa, sitting on the other side of the fire, and looking as though all the cares of the world were on her shoulders. She was well used to Vanessa's inhibitions with anyone who was unwell, to the fact that she simply could not be natural with them; and wondered if she was so deeply troubled now because Justin was so much more important to her than anyone else in the world. Or was there any other reason?

Her own feeling about Justin, and the need to conceal it, put a brake on Amanda's normal frankness, but after a while she could endure the unexplained gloom no longer. She shut her book with a bang. 'What *is* the matter, Vanessa? Are you worrying just because you can't help being stiff with sick people? Or is there anything else?'

Vanessa gave her a startled look. 'I don't know what to do,' she said, looking guilty, shame-faced, and rather childish. 'I've made the most terrible mistake.'

Amanda looked at her in silence for a few moments, then asked, with a calmness that astonished herself: 'Do you mean that you don't really want to marry Justin?'

'Yes,' said Vanessa. They gazed at one another in silence again, then she added on a rising note of desperation: 'What can I do? I can't tell Justin I want to break it off now, while he's not well. It would be brutal.'

'But do you have to do anything in a hurry? Surely it would be better to wait, and think it over? When did you begin to change your mind?'

'The afternoon I first went to see Justin in hospital. No, before that, when everyone took it for granted that I must be his first visitor. I didn't want to go and see him.'

Amanda stared down at her fingers, and her feelings were chaotic, pulling her first in one direction, then in the other. She forced herself to look at Vanessa's tragic face. 'If your feelings seemed to change, only because Justin was in hospital,' she said slowly, 'don't you think it's a purely temporary thing? You don't *like* people when they're ill. You wouldn't come and see me, when I had my appendix out. You spent the whole of your pocket money buying presents for me, but would hardly come inside my room, when I came out of hospital. If you changed only when Justin got hurt, I think that's what has made you feel differently. Things will probably right themselves, once he's well again; so surely it would be a mistake to say anything now?'

Vanessa shook her head dolefully. 'I wish I could think that. No, you were right in the very beginning, when you accused me of play-acting. I know I was furious, but I wonder if that was because I knew there was some truth in it, but wouldn't admit it.' Amanda looked at her silently, her thoughts in confusion. A few months ago, she would not have been in the least surprised by this confession, but she had gradually come to believe that Vanessa was genuinely in love with Justin. 'I suppose you'll think I've been a complete fool,' Vanessa went on, desperation in her voice. 'I can't explain it, even to myself. I suppose it was partly Richard. He dropped me for another girl, a student at the same university, and I was utterly miserable. Oh, I know I've never admitted that, but it's true. Then, when we came up here, you were away most of the time, and I was dreadfully lonely. The Warrens took me up, and I suppose I was flattered. They were quite different from anyone I'd ever known before, and Danesford so lovely. When I met Justin, I really believed I was in love with him, but now — '

'Do you mean you were not in love with Justin himself, but just a glamorous picture — lovely house, long pedigree, and yourself a part of it?'

'I suppose so. But I am fond of Justin. I don't want to hurt him. But I don't want to marry him. What am I to do?' wailed Vanessa.

'Is Justin in love with you?'

'Oh, yes,' answered Vanessa, with a complete confidence Amanda could have done without. 'That's what makes it so awful. I only wish he wasn't.'

'Then you can't tell him until he's well enough to take it,' said Amanda, with decision. 'And I still think it would be better to wait, for your own sake. You may feel quite differently when he's out of hospital.'

'No, I won't,' returned Vanessa obstinately. 'And the longer I put it off the worse it will be. No, I'm not just being gloomy. Think of all those expensive alterations to Northbrook! We'd agreed that Justin should pay for any repairs, but I'd pay for all the fancy alterations I wanted. How can I let them go on with the work? Do you think Justin would still let me pay for it, if I refuse to marry him?'

'Gosh! I hadn't thought of that,' exclaimed Amanda. 'No, I'm pretty sure he wouldn't.'

'But he never wanted them, and can't afford to pay for them. Do you think I really ought to go on with my engagement?'

'Just because of money complications, no I don't,' said Amanda firmly.

'Caroline Warren might make some sort of success of a marriage without love, but you wouldn't.'

'Frankly, I can't think of any worse nightmare than being married to the wrong man.' The note of desperation was back in Vanessa's voice. 'I've only just begun to realize I don't even know Justin very well. But I am fond of him. He's always been sweet to me, and I don't want to make him unhappy.'

'If you were unhappy, you'd probably make him even more unhappy, in the long run. It may be difficult to break an engagement, but much easier than to break a marriage.'

'Why aren't you saying I told you so?'

'That would be a fat lot of help,' retorted Amanda impatiently. 'I suppose Justin thinks you're in love with him?'

'Well, of course. I believed it myself, until a week ago, so why should he doubt it?'

Why indeed? thought Amanda. Vanessa had acted the part well enough to have convinced her, in the end, and she had a much longer and more intimate experience of Vanessa's temperament than Justin. They sat in silence for some time, each following their separate thoughts. Then Amanda asked: 'What about Richard, Vanessa? Do you still love him, or was that just play-acting, too?'

'I don't know.' Again Vanessa's voice verged on desperation. 'I thought I was in love with him. But I've believed for months that I was in love with Justin, and I wasn't, not really. How can I feel sure of anything, now? And what does it matter? It was Richard who tired of me.'

'No. If he sheered off, it was only because he was afraid of being thought a fortune-hunter. I've sometimes wondered if Mother warned him off.' Vanessa gave her a very startled look, but said nothing. 'I saw him in July, and I'd swear he was still in love with you.' Vanessa still said nothing. Amanda looked at her bent, dark head, and wondered how much disappointment and hurt pride had contributed to her foolish engagement; whether she had unconsciously wanted to *show* Richard that she could do without him, and make a much grander match. She had suspected this, in the beginning.

'If I could, I'd like to see Richard again,' said Vanessa at last. 'If I could see him, talk to him, perhaps I'd know what I really feel about him. But right now, I feel as though I can never be sure of myself again. And anyway, I'm still engaged to Justin. I don't see how I can go on with it, nor how I can break it off. If it wasn't for the money, even! I feel bad about jilting him, but then to land him with a walloping big bill for alterations he never wanted! I don't think I can do that. And you keep on saying, don't do anything in a hurry. How do you think I can go and see him each day, and pretend that everything is exactly the same?'

'As you've acted a part very success-fully for months, surely you can keep it up for a bit longer?'

'That was different. I honestly believed

I was in love with Justin. Now, I know I'm not. Everything's different. Justin will soon begin to realize something's wrong. And I simply cannot go and see him again tomorrow, after all this.'

Amanda looked at Vanessa's tear-stained face, and felt sincerely sorry for her. She might have been silly, but she was certainly paying for it. 'Get Mother to ring up and say you've got a headache, or a cold, and can't come for a day or two.'

'But he'll be dreadfully disappointed. Amanda, would you go, instead of me, and tell him I'm not well? Better still, would you tell him I can't marry him?'

'Me!' exclaimed Amanda. Vanessa looked at her pleadingly, but she shook her head. 'No, Vanessa. I've pulled plenty of your chestnuts out of the fire in the past, but that's asking too much. You owe it to Justin to tell him yourself. If I did it for you, he'd think you were afraid of him.'

'I'm not afraid of Justin, but I am afraid of hurting him. And of looking a fool,' added Vanessa, almost inaudibly. 'And you could do it much better than me.'

Vanessa little knew that she was about the worst person in the world to convey such a message, thought Amanda. 'If Justin loves you, then no one can do it well.'

'At least, go and see him tomorrow, and tell him I've got a bad headache.'

'I don't know. I'll think about it.'

Amanda picked up her book, but used it only as a screen for her own thoughts. If Vanessa did not marry Justin, she could not be wholly sorry. She would be spared the pain of seeing them constantly together. But on the other hand, she hated to think that Justin might be hurt. She had never been convinced that he was truly in love with Vanessa, but she could have been wrong. Justin was not a man to display his feelings to the whole world. If he did love Vanessa, he would be doubly hurt, in his affection for her, and his love for Danesford. Even the minor matter of paying for the alterations to Northbrook would hit him quite hard, particularly when he had promised to pay for the improvements at Staneshiel.

It was often difficult, even for someone who knew her as well as Amanda, to disentangle the real Vanessa from the fantasy one. At first, Amanda had more than half believed that Vanessa's doubts would vanish, when Justin was completely recovered. But she could not believe that Vanessa was play-acting now. She was far too miserable and upset. Amanda had always felt that Vanessa was in love with Richard, so it was easier for her to believe that she had only been trying to find a satisfactory substitute in Justin. Being Vanessa, she had thrown herself into the role so whole-heartedly that she had succeeded in convincing herself, and everyone else, of its genuiness.

And what about me? Amanda asked herself, and could find no comforting answers. She had no reason to believe that Justin would ever learn to love her. All her belief in a unity of thought and feeling between them vanished. She was very much afraid that Vanessa was right in her certainty that Justin was in love with her. She was in the best position to know, after all. And even if, as Amanda suspected, Danesford was Justin's chief love, he would have a bitter disappointment there, too.

Before the evening was over, Vanessa had persuaded her to go to the hospital in her place, next morning. Amanda was not quite sure why she agreed. She was sorry for Vanessa, who had muddled herself into a very unenviable situation, and wanted to oblige her. And perhaps she could not resist the opportunity to see Justin, in spite of the inevitable awkwardness. But she remained unpersuadable in her refusal to do Vanessa's explaining for her. If she told Justin that Vanessa had a cold, that would give her a few days in which to pull herself together. Then she could go and see him again, and decide on the best time to reveal her change of heart.

Amanda could take an enviably cool

head into an examination room, but now her heart was involved, not her head, and her imagination worked overtime. As she left, Vanessa said: 'You'd better give Justin my love, and if an opportunity should crop up — '

'No,' said Amanda, very firmly.

Arrived at the hospital, she went slowly up the stairs, tense with apprehension. It was a relief to find that Randall was with Justin. They broke off their conversation, when Amanda appeared. She explained about Vanessa's headache, and sat down, a little way from the other two, telling them to carry on, and not mind her. They took her at her word, and continued discussing details about the running of the farm, and Amanda could study Justin, unobserved. He was up, sitting in an easy chair, clad in a dressing-gown, his right arm in a sling. His face was a little thinner than before, and still pale, but Amanda thought he looked remarkably fit, considering everything, and in good spirits.

After about ten minutes, Randall got

up to go, and all Amanda's nervousness came flooding back again. When he had gone, she turned quickly and nervously to Justin. 'How's Randall doing at the farm?'

'He's doing a very good job, and plans to come and live with me there, once I can get away from here. We can go home for one meal a day. This arm of mine won't be really serviceable for some time yet, so Randall says he'll go on helping until after Christmas, and then look around for a job elsewhere.'

'Oh, I *am* glad!' exclaimed Amanda, losing a good deal of her awkwardness in interest.

'Now that Randall has decided to bury the hatchet, there would be plenty of room for both of us at Danesford,' said Justin slowly. 'We could never have worked together, before this. If he'd taken over the management of the estate, his first object would have been to make things more difficult for me. And if I'd proposed turning Ridley's and Northbrook into one unit, and

Randall's helping to run it, he'd never have taken orders from me. We'd have clashed continuously. But I still think it's better for him to get a job away from home for the next year or two. He needs the extra experience, and a couple of years away from his mother's spoiling habits would do him all the good in the world. After that, he can decide if he'd rather work here, and in what way.'

'I've always thought he'd be happier, if he was really independent,' agreed Amanda.

Justin gave her a quick, keen glance. 'What's the matter with Vanessa?' he asked abruptly.

Amanda caught her breath. 'I told you,' she answered very carefully. 'She's got a bad headache, and thought she was starting with a cold. She really wasn't fit to come.'

Justin made an impatient gesture with his good arm. 'That's not what I meant, and I'm quite sure you know it isn't. Vanessa's been running away from me all week, and I would like to know why.'

His eyes met and held Amanda's. She felt trapped, but put up a determined defence. 'I'm afraid that's just Vanessa's way, when people are ill. She's no good with sick people, even people she loves. They almost frighten her. I've always thought it went back to her father's death. She was only eight. He was ill for a long time, and I think it's made her scared of all illness.'

'Do I look ill, now? Or act ill?' demanded Justin, his eyes fixed on Amanda's face, as though trying to read her thoughts. 'Come to that, Vanessa's not the only one who's acting scared of me. You are, and that's much more remarkable. Has Vanessa changed her mind about marrying me?'

Amanda's defences crumbled. She found that she could not give a direct lie to Justin. 'Yes,' she admitted. 'She broke down last night, and told me she couldn't go on with it. She was dreadfully upset. She said she was very fond of you, but didn't think she had ever been really in love with you, though she had managed to convince herself that she was.'

'She certainly convinced me,' commented Justin, dryly.

Amanda's eyes searched his face, trying to find some clue to his feelings, but not succeeding. 'She was too upset to come and see you,' she went on, trying to explain and excuse Vanessa. 'It's not so much that she's changed her mind, as that she's been living in a sort of make-believe. Before we came up here, there was someone I thought she was in love with. He was a medical student, with nothing but his grant, and when Vanessa inherited all that money, he let himself be frightened off. Vanessa insisted that they'd just got tired of each other, but I always thought she'd been quite badly hurt. When we moved, Vanessa was lonely, and missing Richard. Then you came along, and she liked you, and she got a bit beglamoured by Danesford, and family tradition, and all that. I don't want you to think that she accepted

271

you in cold blood, because of those things,' she added hastily. 'Vanessa's got a very romantic imagination, and they added enormously to your attraction. Then your accident was a shock to her, and it seems to have had the odd effect of wakening her from a dream. I thought she'd change again, once you were out again, but now, I don't really think she will.'

'I see,' said Justin. Amanda looked at him with an unspoken question in her eyes. 'You never believed *I* was in love with Vanessa, did you?' he added. Amanda felt the blood flame into her face, and could find no words. 'Well, I didn't plan cold-bloodedly to marry her for her assets, either. Vanessa's lovely enough to please any man. I liked her, and she showed pretty plainly that she liked me. At twenty-seven, I'd never been whole-heartedly in love. I told myself that the affection I felt for Vanessa was enough, that few people could hope for more. But, in my heart, I think I knew more clearly than

Vanessa what I was doing. Danesford has always meant too much to me. It's bedevilled my relations with Randall. I deliberately blinded myself to my strongest motive, until you came on the scene. You looked at me with such scornful accusation. No matter how much I justified myself, it was always there, stripping me of comforting illusions.'

He broke off, and looked at her, and it seemed to Amanda that his eyes were now doing the real talking, only she did not dare to believe what they seemed to be saying. 'I've no excuse for what I did,' Justin went on, 'except that I suppose we've all been one sort of fool or another, at some time. And I'd never learnt how much difference there is between attraction and real love; not until I knew you.' He looked at her in a way that made her heart turn right over. She jumped to her feet, and went straight to him. Justin's good arm went round her, drawing her down on to the arm of his chair, and holding her close. They looked at one another in a wondering uncertainty, and then their lips met in a long kiss, which wiped out all Amanda's doubts. She looked at him in speechless joy. 'When I kept on trying to justify myself to you,' said Justin slowly, 'I thought it was just pride, that I hated you to think I was marrying for money. When I realized why I hated it so much, it seemed pretty hopeless. I was engaged to Vanessa, and I thought she loved me. But this last week, I've wondered if she'd begun to change, and I couldn't forget the night you stayed with me, up on the hill.'

'Did you hear what I said to you, then?'

'No; what did you say?'

'I don't really remember myself. But I think some of it was quite revealing. I thought you were unconscious, and couldn't hear. But I've wondered since.'

'Perhaps something got through. When I came round here, it was to an overpowering impression that you'd been with me, but now you'd gone. All I had was a yawning emptiness, that I'd

have to live with for the rest of my life.'
His arm tightened about her. 'This is
when I could do with two good arms.'

'You're not doing badly with one,'
Amanda laughed. She rested her cheek
against his, and they sat together in a
happiness that seemed to need no words.

'Will you marry me?' asked Justin, at
length.

'I've got no money, you know.'

'Don't rub it in!'

'I wasn't; only warning you.' Amanda
rushed to justify herself, but with laughter in her eyes. 'I've not got a penny,
and you've got to think about your farm,
and the future.'

'And I warn you that it won't be easy.
But I doubt if you want everything easy.
Will you marry me, or won't you?'

'Of course I will,' answered Amanda,
even more hastily than before. Then
added: 'But not for a while yet.'

'Well, no, perhaps not. The sooner
the better, as far as I'm concerned, but
you'll want to get your degree, after
putting so much work into it. And I

don't want a wife in Newcastle, while I have to be here.'

'I think it would be better to get my degree,' agreed Amanda. 'But it was Vanessa I was thinking about.'

Justin's eyebrows shot up in surprise. 'From what you said, I thought Vanessa would be very relieved to be quit of me.'

'I think she will be. But if you got engaged to someone else, the minute you were free, how could she help thinking you never cared for her, but only for her money? She thinks she's made an absolute fool of herself, believing she was in love when she wasn't, and at the moment she seems to have lost all confidence in herself. Her pride took a bad knock when Richard deserted her, and I don't want to give it another. If I could bring her and Richard together, first.'

'Do you think she still loves him?'

'I'm not sure, and neither is she. I am sure that Richard still loves her, and Vanessa isn't nearly as changeable as she can seem. I have a feeling that, deep down, she's never stopped loving him. If they could meet again,' Amanda said slowly, thinking aloud. 'But not here. Mother doesn't think he's a good enough match for Vanessa. I might ring him up, but I couldn't do it from home.'

'Then use my telephone at Ridley's. I'd like Vanessa to be happy, too. I am fond of her, you know. And grateful,' he added, with a faint twinkle. 'It beats me, Amanda, why you should care about me, after seeing the hash I've made of my engagement; and with Randall.'

'Oh, well, if we're going to be so modest,' said Amanda blithely. 'I'd better warn you that I'm bossy, meddlesome, opinionated, obstinate, and reckless. Ask Vanessa; but you probably know it already.'

Justin looked at her, and then he began to whistle softly. Amanda's eyes widened, as she recognized the tune again. 'That's the Fair Flower of Northumberland! When you whistled it in the cottage, you were thinking of real flowers, surely?'

'No, only of one girl. That wet

afternoon in the cottage, you in bare feet, and that Aran pullover, your wet hair turning red in the firelight, finished me. I'd suspected it before, but I knew that for me you were the one fair flower of Northumberland, and I hadn't the remotest hope of winning you. We never seemed to stop arguing; but talking together over the map that day, I felt that we could be truly at one in mind and heart, in a way that I'd never known before. Our life won't be easy, I've told you that, but I still believe we can be at one, through the good and the bad, don't you?'

'Oh, yes,' agreed Amanda fervently, and kissed him with a passion of tenderness.

When she finally tore herself away, Justin provided her with a key to Ridley's, and a convenient excuse for returning in the afternoon. When Amanda reached home, Vanessa came into the hall, and gave her a questioning look. 'Come upstairs with me,' said Amanda. She busied herself taking off coat and shoes, so as to keep her face partly hidden, as she talked. 'I told you I wouldn't tell Justin you wanted to break off your engagement, but I had to. He asked me.'

'He asked you!'

'Yes.' Amanda stooped to untie her shoes. 'He knew something was wrong, and thought it might be easier to get a straight answer from me. I tried to put him off, at first, but in the end I thought the truth would be best.' She looked up to meet Vanessa's startled eyes. 'You've nothing to worry about, Vanessa. He took it very well.'

A variety of expressions chased each other across Vanessa's face. 'Do you mean that he didn't really mind? That he was only marrying me for my money, after all?'

'No, I do not,' said Amanda swiftly. 'If it was your money he wanted, he'd be pretty disappointed at losing it, wouldn't he? Take it from me, Justin's very fond of you. But he'd been worried at the way you'd been acting, suspected that you wanted to call off your engagement, and then begun to ask himself if either of you loved the other quite enough for marriage. Surely you'd rather he was regretful, but not exactly heartbroken?'

'Yes,' said Vanessa uncertainly. Then relief began to grow in her face. 'Oh, yes, of course I would.'

'Well, I know I would. You won't mind going to see him, and getting everything straightened out between you, now?'

'No; but not today. He doesn't expect me to come today, does he? I'd like a day or two first.'

'He wants some books and oddments from Ridley's, but I can take them, if you'd rather. He knows you're upset, and have a headache. But I'd go and see him tomorrow. You've no need to worry about it.'

'It's easy for you to say that. I'm worried about who's going to pay for all the alterations at Northbrook. That's not just a trifle.'

'Oh!' Amanda was brushing her hair.

She stopped short, and it flashed across her mind that now there was an easy answer to this awkward matter. Justin would never let Vanessa pay for the alterations. But, later on, if Vanessa liked to give those improvements to Amanda, as a wedding-present, he could surely not object to that, particularly if it eased Vanessa's conscience. 'It's not a trifle, but it is a detail,' she said firmly. 'Justin can surely stop some of the work, and get the rest finished more cheaply? I should leave it for the present, and settle it later.'

'I don't know. Mother will be terribly disappointed. I don't know what on earth she'll say.'

Amanda put down her brush, and eyed Vanessa with amused sympathy. 'I'm sure she'll say plenty, but you can't marry someone you don't love, just to save her from being disappointed. Anyway, why stay and listen to it all? If I were you, Vanessa, I'd go and see Justin tomorrow. Tell Mother in the evening, and then come and join me in

Newcastle, until it blows over. I'm sure Mrs Cuthbert would let you have her spare room again. I'll ask her, and then give you a ring in the evening.'

'There's nothing I'd like better,' said Vanessa fervently.

The short winter daylight had faded into darkness, when Amanda drove home, after spending the afternoon with Justin. As soon as she had a chance to be alone with Vanessa, she said: 'Justin's expecting you tomorrow afternoon. And when I went over to the farm for his books, I rang up Richard.' Vanessa's face flamed into scarlet, then the blood ebbed away, leaving her very pale. She said nothing. 'I told him you'd broken off your engagement to Justin, and meant to come and spend a week or two with me in Newcastle. I said that, if he would like to see you again, it would be much more comfortable to meet there than here. He jumped at the chance, and said if I'd book a room for him, he'd come for the week-end.'

'You didn't tell him that I still — '
Vanessa's voice faltered and stopped.

'I told him nothing, and promised
nothing,' said Amanda firmly. 'I said
that you were feeling unhappy, and not
quite sure of anything; but you had said
you would like to see him, as a friend.'

'But are you sure he *wants* to come?'

'Am I sure! Listen, Vanessa, this is
the middle of term for him. He's
probably up to his eyes in work. But
he'll give up a long week-end, without a
second's thought, just to see you again.
That may not mean much to you, but
I know how to rate it. I tell you, he
leaped at the chance, without even
stopping to think. It's my belief that
Richard's learnt that you can pay too
high a price for pride, and wishes he
hadn't let you go so easily. I thought
that last summer, and I'm quite sure of
it now. You do want to see him again,
don't you?'

'Oh, yes; more than anything else.'

'Well, perhaps it was interfering of me
to ring him without asking you; but I

wanted to be able to tell you his reaction to the suggestion. And I promise not to interfere any further, but to leave you to work it out together,' Amanda finished.

She looked at the little glow of happiness that had come into Vanessa's eyes, and smiled. This arrangement would mean that she would have to stay in Newcastle next week-end, when she longed to come back and see Justin again, but she thought it would be well worth that small sacrifice. When she thought of the apprehension and unhappiness with which she had looked forward to the Christmas vacation, and then of the change that one day had made, she was filled with incredulous joy.

THE END

Other titles in the
Linford Romance Library:

SURGEON IN PORTUGAL

Anna Ramsay

'A strong dose of sunshine' is the prescription for Nurse Liz Larking, recovering from glandular fever. And a villa in the Algarve seems the ideal place to recuperate, even if it means cooking for the villa's owner, eminent cardiac surgeon Hugh Forsythe: brilliant, caring, awe-inspiring — and dangerously easy to fall in love with. Liz soon realises that this doctor is more potent than any virus — and ironically, it seems he could just as easily break a heart as cure one . . .

CINDERELLA SRN

Anna Ramsay

Despite her tender years, Student Nurse Kate Cameron is like a mother hen, forever worrying about her patients and her family. So it's a huge joke when her friends transform her into a *femme fatale* for the hospital's Christmas Ball. The joke backfires though, when Kate finds herself falling in love . . . But what chance is there of a fairy-tale ending when this Cinderella has chapped hands and an unflattering uniform, and Prince Charming turns out to be Luke Harvey, the new senior registrar?

A VERY SPECIAL GIRL

Renee Shann

Though warned by her parents, Emma marries Nicholas Stagger, a Krasnovian from Traj. Too late she has found that her parents were right, for Nicky's infidelities are more than she can stand. Furthermore, Nicky's involvement in the politics of his own country brings Emma herself into danger; but it is through this involvement that she meets Paul, President of Krasnovia. At last Emma can see her future clearly, but danger still awaits . . .

NORTH BY NORTHEAST

Phyllis Humphrey

Haley Parsons, a school teacher on her first real vacation in years, boards the beautiful and luxurious American Orient Express for a week-long train excursion from New Orleans to Washington, D.C. But then her jewelry begins to disappear and she finds herself an unwitting player in a kidnapping and robbery attempt. The culprit is evidently aboard the train; and Jonathan Shafer, Haley's handsome, newfound love interest, is somehow involved. Who is he, really? And what part will he play in all this?

A TEMPORARY LOVER

Carol Wood

Sophie Shaw had taken pride and pleasure in building up a veterinary practice with her husband Michael and his partner, but Michael's death had left a void in her life. It seemed none of the applicants for the practice was right — until Luke Jordon pointed out that *she* was the problem. Once Luke began his duties, Sophie had to admit that he was an excellent vet, but he also raised a frisson in her that had nothing to do with work . . .